"Do you think we could be friends, Sarah?"

Anton's stern features relaxed into a disarming smile as he asked the question.

Her name sounded strange on his lips, and a curious sensation spiraled through her, leaving her feeling oddly weak. Could they be friends? No, never.

"I've been told it's not wise to become too friendly with one's doctor." She deliberately evaded his query. "Patients are inclined to reveal too many secrets to their doctors that might make it awkward for them to indulge later in a normal relationship."

"If you have secrets, Sarah Courtney," he said, "you're not the kind of woman to divulge them to anyone unless you felt driven to it."

It startled her that he could have summed her up so accurately—but why should she somehow feel as if she'd been severely rebuked?

YVONNE WHITTAL, a born dreamer, started scribbling stories at an early age but admits she's glad she didn't have to make her living by writing then. "Otherwise," she says, "I would surely have starved!" After her marriage and the birth of three daughters, she began submitting short stories to publishers. Now she derives great satisfaction from writing full-lengh books. The characters become part of Yvonne's life in the process, so much so that she almost hates coming to the end of each manuscript and having to say farewell to dear and trusted friends.

Books by Yvonne Whittal

HARLEQUIN PRESENTS

HARLEQUIN ROMANCE

YVONNE WHITTAL

shadow across the moon

Harlequin Books

TORONTO • NEW YORK • LONDON
AMSTERDAM • PARIS • SYDNEY • HAMBURG
STOCKHOLM • ATHENS • TOKYO • MILAN

Harlequin Presents first edition April 1991
ISBN 0-373-11358-7

Original hardcover edition published in 1990
by Mills & Boon Limited

SHADOW ACROSS THE MOON

CHAPTER ONE

THE Boeing was making its descent through the blanket of clouds to Johannesburg's Jan Smuts Airport when Sarah Courtney made her way cautiously down the aisle, and the grey-haired man seated at the window turned his head to look at her as she sat down beside him and fastened her seatbelt with hands which were not as steady as she would have wished.

Ivor Shaw studied his god-daughter intently, his dark eyes taking in her slender elegance in the cream linen suit and green silk blouse which was open at the throat to reveal a single string of pearls. Sarah projected an image of cool sophistication with her rich auburn hair swept back from her classic features into a stylish chignon, and her businesslike attire heightened rather than quelled her femininity, but that was not what Ivor was thinking about while he studied her attractive profile.

'You're terribly pale, Sarah,' he remarked, his bushy eyebrows meeting in a worried frown. 'Aren't you feeling well?'

Her tawny eyes met his and, just for a moment, they revealed an inner discomfort before the corners of her freshly painted mouth lifted in a wry smile. 'I think I must have eaten something which doesn't agree with me.'

Ivor accepted her explanation with a sympathetic murmur, but Sarah had not told her godfather the truth. She had not been feeling well for some weeks now, but she had never before experienced anything quite as bad as this. The unfamiliar quickening of her pulses had brought on a rush of clammy anxiety, and she had come close to fainting that morning shortly before she had had to step on to the podium to deliver the opening address at the new branch of Courtney's in Bloemfontein.It had been a frightening experience which she had hoped would not be repeated, but that sensation had recurred a few minutes ago in the confined space of the toilet while she had been washing her hands and touching up her lipstick before they landed at Jan Smuts. This time, however, it had left her with a nagging headache and a peculiar feeling of physical exhaustion to contend with.

It was October, mid-spring in the southern hemisphere, and the clouds gathering in the sky promised rain when the Boeing landed a few minutes later. The breeze blowing across the tarmac whipped the colour back into Sarah's cheeks as they walked briskly towards the airport building. It was not cold, but for some obscure reason she was shivering uncontrollably and her fingers tightened unconsciously about the handle of her briefcase.

She was uncommonly tense while they waited in the crowded arrival hall to collect their overnight bags,and it was only when they were settled in the warm, comfortable interior of the chauffeur-driven Mercedes that she began to relax again.

She reached for the receiver of the car telephone and punched out a number while her godfather watched her with a disapproving look on his leathery face, but Sarah chose to ignore that look for the moment when Lois Beecham answered the call in her clear, precise voice.

'We're on our way to the store, Lois,' Sarah informed her secretary with a note of cool authority in her husky voice. 'Tell Steve de Vos that I want him in my office the minute we arrive, and I want you there as well, Lois. I'd like to catch up on what's been happening while I've been away.'

Sarah ended the conversation as abruptly as it had begun, then she leaned back in her seat with a faint smile curving her generous mouth and directed her amused gaze at the man seated beside her.

'Why do I get the feeling lately that my actions are meeting with your disapproval?' she demanded with her usual candour, but disapproval mingled with concern in the dark eyes that met hers.

'This meeting with Steve and Lois could have waited until morning, Sarah, and I don't approve of the relentless way you've been driving yourself lately.'

Sarah's dark, perfectly arched brows rose above clear, mocking eyes. 'I'm what you've made of me, Ivor, and you know as well as I do that the work preceding the opening of a new branch of Courtney's is a mere trifle compared to the work which must follow to ensure that we succeed in our objective.'

'I'm aware of the work involved in such a project, Sarah, but I also happen to be worried about you.' He sighed irritably and reached for her unnaturally cold hand to clasp it tightly with his warm fingers. 'You *will* persist in driving yourself to the limit, and it's so unnecessary when you have in your employ a capable young assistant like Steve de Vos who's more than ready to shoulder some of the responsibility if only you'd give him the opportunity.'

Sarah could not argue with that. Steve de Vos was a man of about her own age, and he had come to Courtney's almost direct from university. He was enterprising, ambitious,and more than capable of coping with a large share of her workload, but she continued to guard her position jealously, afraid that if she relinquished her task she might find herself floundering without the stability of the only anchor she possessed.

'Taking charge of Courtney's has become a way of life to me over the years, and I enjoy what I'm doing,' she defended herself.

'You're twenty-seven, my dear, and for the past six years you've unstintingly dedicated yourself to making your father's dream for Courtney's a reality.' Ivor delivered this reminder sombrely. 'What you've done is commendable, and no one knows that better than I do. You're Sarah Courtney, and you've won nation-wide acclaim as the illustrious head of the chain of Courtney's stores throughout the country. Your name is on everyone's lips; in the clothing industry it's synonymous with the very latest fashion and style, and I seldom pick up a newspaper or a magazine these days without seeing your face on one of its pages. But what about Sarah Courtney the *woman*?'

Ivor's query stabbed at a sensitive core, and Sarah turned her face away to stare blindly through the tinted window at the flow of traffic into the city. 'I find my job rewarding and fulfilling.'

'I'm not talking about your *business* life, I'm talking about your *private* life, and you know it, Sarah,' he rebuked her censoriously, ignoring that steely, forbidding note he had detected in her husky voice.

'My business life and my private life are one.'

'That's exactly what I mean!' Ivor exploded, secure

in the knowledge that the chauffeur's loyalty to Sarah would prevent him from repeating their conversation. 'You need a man in your life, and, if marriage doesn't feature on your agenda for the future, then I suggest you occasionally settle for a passionate affair.'

Sarah's mouth quirked humorously, but the soft laughter that spilled briefly from her coral-pink lips was tainted with a touch of bitterness as she turned in her seat to face the man who was, not only her godfather, but her chief accountant and mentor. 'I shall never marry again,' she stated firmly, 'and I have neither the time nor the inclination for an affair, passionate or otherwise!'

Ivor sighed exasperatedly, but he knew better than to pursue the subject, and they lapsed into a thoughtful silence which neither of them made any attempt to break during the remainder of the drive to the Courtney's store in the centre of the city.

Sarah's office on the tenth floor was a spacious room with wood-panelled walls and a large window over-looking the supreme court. The air-conditioner sent a steady flow of regulated air into the office, but Sarah was feeling strangely chilled as she sat behind her large mahogany desk, and her glance briefly followed Ivor when he got up to pour himself a drink from the well-stocked cabinet in the matching mahogany wall unit.

Her godfather had been correct in saying that this meeting could have waited until morning. For the past hour or more she had listened attentively, she had made notes and she had commented on what Lois Beecham and Steve de Vos had had to tell her, but she was experiencing again the unfamiliar surge of clammy anxiety and the uncomfortable acceleration of her pulse-rate which had, twice before that day, brought her close to fainting

'A telex came through from the factory in Cape Town,' Lois Beecham was saying, unaware of the silent and desperate battle Sarah was fighting against that blanket of darkness which threatened to engulf her. 'It appears that there'll be a two-month delay in the delivery of the consignment of silk we ordered from the East, and the couturier is in a bit of a flap about having the garments ready for next year's autumn collection.'

Lois glanced at Steve de Vos, and he nodded his sleek fair head as if to confirm her statement while he passed a file across the desk towards Sarah. 'I managed to purchase a considerable batch of silk locally. It's all there in the file, and I'm sure you'll agree that it ought to tide us through until the consignment arrives.'

'Good work, Steve,' Sarah complimented him, moistening her dry lips with the tip of her tongue as she glanced with a measure of impatience at the slim gold watch strapped to her slender wrist.

It was long after five. She could hear the muted sound of the late afternoon traffic in the street below and, directing her gaze at her secretary, she said, 'You may go, Lois, and I'm sorry to have kept you so late.'

Lois Beecham was in her early forties, and after five years as Sarah's secretary she had become accustomed to working long and irregular hours. Sarah's apologies were always sincere, and Lois always accepted them with a gracious, often humorous smile, but on this occasion her expression was unnaturally grave as she rose to her feet.

She said goodnight to Ivor and Steve, but as she passed behind Sarah's chair she paused to murmur, 'If you'll forgive me saying so, Miss Courtney, you're not looking well, and it might do you good to have a couple of early nights.'

Lois Beecham did not expect a response to her statement, and neither did Sarah give her one as she leaned back in her chair to watch her secretary walk out of her office and close the door firmly behind her.

A couple of early nights? Sarah almost laughed out loud at the suggestion. She would give anything to have an early night, but sleep was a commodity which had been evading her persistently during the past weeks.

It was raining heavily. She watched the raindrops gathering and running in little rivulets down the large window panes, then she turned her attention back to Ivor and Steve. She could see them locked in conversation, but for a moment she could not hear what they were saying, and she wondered frantically why her concentration was slipping so badly lately.

The fog clouding her mind finally cleared and she heard her godfather asking Steve, 'How soon can we have the Bloemfontein branch linked up on computer?'

'There's been some stupid delay, but I've been assured that they'll be linked up by the end of the week.'

Sarah was beginning to feel oddly dismembered while she sat there picking up only snatches of the ensuing discussion. Their voices seemed to fade and clear like a bad telephone connection, but it was not until their features became distorted in a peculiar mist that she rose abruptly to her feet.

I need a drink, she thought, rising abruptly behind her desk, and that was the last thing she remembered until she found herself lying on the leather couch in her office with Steve de Vos's anxious face peering down at her.

'What happened?' she croaked, aware of her godfather's low, gruff voice speaking into the telephone on her desk as she lowered her feet to the floor and sat up, but that was a mistake. 'Oh, God, I feel awful!' she groaned, one hand clutching at her heaving stomach and the other at her dizzy, aching head.

'You fainted,' Steve explained in a lowered, anxious voice. 'Mr Shaw is arranging for you to see a doctor at the medical centre.'

Sarah dropped her hands into her lap, her eyes dark and a little wild in her pale face. 'I don't need a doctor!'

'You may not think so, but you're nevertheless going to see one,' Ivor announced authoritatively, dropping the telephone receiver on to its cradle and walking towards her with her raincoat in his hands. 'Anton is waiting for you at his rooms, so let's not keep him waiting longer than is necessary.'

'No doctor in his right mind would see a patient at this hour of the day,' she argued, digging her fingers into the leather couch as she lowered herself cautiously on to her feet, and she sighed inwardly with relief when her unsteady legs managed to support the weight of her body. 'And who is this . . .er . . .Anton, anyway?' she demanded irritably.

'His name is Anton de Ville, he's an excellent physician, and his father was once a very good friend of mine.' Ivor's glance was speculative as he looked down into Sarah's pale, angry face. 'Are you going to come willingly, or do I have to drag you to his rooms at the medical centre?'

Steve de Vos eyed the two people who stood locked in silent battle, then he cleared his throat self-consciously. 'Well, I still have a few urgent matters to see to in my office before I go home, so I'll say goodnight.'

Sarah nodded, her throat too dry to speak for the moment, but Ivor glanced at her young assistant and smiled briefly. 'Thanks for your help, Steve.'

Steve de Vos nodded, his concerned glance darting swiftly at Sarah before he walked out of the office and left her alone with her godfather.

She did not want to see a doctor . . .not *yet* anyway. She was not ready for it, and it was unfair of Ivor to spring it on her like this.

'I feel fine now, and I don't——'

'Do it for me, Sarah,' Ivor interrupted her angry protest. 'I'm worried about you. As a matter of fact I've been worried about you for a long time now, and it would set my mind at rest knowing you've seen a doctor.'

'You worry too much,' she grumbled, but her resistance fled when she looked up into her godfather's concerned face, and she slipped her arms obligingly into the coat he held out for her.

Ivor's wife had died many years ago, and Sarah was to him the child he had never had. He worried and fretted over her in a way her own father had never done, and Sarah loved him for it despite her argumentative resistance to his fatherly concern for her.

The medical centre was no more than a few blocks away from Courtney's, and Ivor insisted on driving her there in her dark green Mercedes. 'I'm not going to risk your passing out behind the wheel,' he explained, 'and

I can always take a taxi from your flat to my own.'

Sarah did not argue with him this time. Her head was aching and she was beginning to feel extraordinarily tired.

There were not many lights on in the medical centre when they arrived there a few minutes later, and Sarah was grateful for her godfather's steadying hand beneath her elbow as he accompanied her into the building.

Dr Anton de Ville's rooms were on the fifth floor, and the unmistakable smell of antiseptics quivered in Sarah's nostrils when they entered the large waiting-room with its glass-topped tables and comfortably padded armchairs. A dark-haired woman in her late thirties rose from behind the steel desk, and the impressively studded epaulettes on the shoulders of her white uniform blinked beneath the overhead lights as she approached Sarah.

'Dr de Ville said I'm to show you in the moment you arrive, Miss Courtney,' she announced with a pleasant smile.

Sarah darted a glance at Ivor, and he knew her well enough to recognise that look of momentary panic in the depths of her tawny eyes.

'There's nothing to it,' he said, smiling as he murmured those half-forgotten words of encouragement, then his fingers tightened briefly on her arm in a gesture of reassurance. 'I'll wait outside in the car.'

Sarah nodded mutely and allowed herself to be ushered into the well-lit consulting-room where a dark-haired, white-coated man stood behind his orderly desk contemplating the city lights beyond the window.

Anton de Ville turned before the nurse could

announce their presence, and his tanned features were set in that professional mask doctors always seemed to wear when confronting a patient.

'That will be all for the moment, Clair.' His voice was deep and velvety. It was soothing and pleasant on the ears, but it also held an unmistakable note of authority, and his nurse retreated, closing the door silently behind her. He subjected Sarah for a moment to his cool, clinical appraisal, then he gestured with a wave of his hand towards the chair on the opposite side of his desk. 'Please sit down, Miss Courtney.'

He waited until she was seated before he lowered his wide-shouldered, lean-hipped frame on to the chair behind his desk. The man was built like an athlete, she thought absently, her nervousness deserting her to some extent as she watched him flick open a file on his desk and pick up his pen.

'How old are you, Miss Courtney?'

She had been unprepared for the nature of that first query. 'Twenty-seven,' she snapped indignantly. 'How old are you?'

'I'm thirty-eight, Miss Courtney, but my age isn't relevant in this instance.'

His stern, firmly chiselled mouth twitched with a suggestion of a smile, and Sarah lowered her gaze hastily to her tightly clenched hands in her lap.

'I'm sorry,' she murmured contritely. 'I've developed a temper lately which I can't seem to control.'

'Have you ever fainted before?' he continued with his probing queries without commenting on her apology.

'No, never,' she answered truthfully.

'Have you ever come close to fainting?' He looked up from the notes he had been making when she failed to answer him. 'Well, have you?'

'Twice,' Sarah confessed reluctantly. 'Once this morning at the official opening of Courtney's in Bloemfontein, and once this afternoon on the flight back to Johannesburg.'

Anton de Ville was certainly not the most good-looking man Sarah had ever met, but there was something about that rugged face with the straight, high-bridged nose and square, resolute jaw that appealed to her, and his dark , neatly trimmed hair had a tendency to curl on to his broad forehead in an attractively boyish manner. He was also a most infuriating man. He fired questions at her, giving no information in return, and she was close to losing her temper again when he rose to his feet and gestured towards the curtained cubicle in the corner of the room.

'Take off your clothes and slip into the robe hanging on a hook against the wall,' he instructed as he strode towards the door. 'I'll send Sister Jarvis in to help you.'

Sarah stepped into the cubicle when the door closed behind him, and Sister Jarvis appeared seconds later to help her out of her clothes. It did not take long to strip down to her lacy bikini panties and, despite the air-conditioned warmth of the room, there were goose-bumps all over her skin when she slipped her arms into the short sleeves of the white clinical robe and turned so that Sister Jarvis could fasten the tapes down her back.

'I'll tell Dr de Ville you're ready.' Sister Jarvis smiled that pleasant smile as she helped Sarah up on to the examination table and draped a light blanket over her legs. 'Just try to relax,' she instructed before she disappeared behind the curtain.

What the hell am I doing here? Sarah asked herself when she was alone, and she was on the verge of succumbing to that rising panic inside her when Anton de Ville stepped around the curtain with Sister Jarvis at his side.

Sarah's last physical check-up was a dim memory of the past, but she did recall that it had not been quite as disturbingly thorough as the examination Anton de Ville was subjecting her to, and not once during the entire examination did his professional mask slip to give her an indication as to his diagnosis.

'Are you perhaps having difficulty sleeping lately?' he asked half an hour later when she was fully dressed once again and seated across the desk from him.

Sarah was forced to recall the many sleepless nights she had endured lately, and she nodded. 'Yes, I am.'

His pen moved rapidly across the small prescription pad, then he tore off the sheet he had written on, and passed it to her across the desk. 'This should help you sleep, and I'd like you back here at eight tomorrow morning for a series of tests.'

Fear clutched at her insides for the first time with an icy hand while she folded the prescription and slipped it into her handbag.

'What's wrong with me?' she demanded sharply, holding his glance with hers, and his stern mouth relaxed once again in a faint smile.

'At the moment you're showing all the symptoms of stress, but more than that I can't say until I have the results of the tests.'

'How long are you going to keep me here tomorrow?' She was thinking about those important meetings she had lined up for the following day, and, when Anton de

Ville took his time answering her, she added impatiently, 'I have a tight schedule to maintain, and I can't simply stay away from the office for an indefinite period of time.'

He nodded with understanding. 'You should be back at the office before lunch, and I'll do my best to have the results here for you by five-thirty tomorrow evening.'

'Thank you.' She rose stiffly from the chair and walked towards the door, but Anton de Ville was there before her.

'I'll get Sister Jarvis to accompany you down in the lift,' he said, opening the door and standing aside for her to pass.

'That won't be necessary.' She looked up then and held his glance for a startled second. He had nice eyes. They were a deep, incredible blue surrounded by dark, enviably long lashes. His straight, heavy eyebrows lifted suddenly in a faintly amused query, and for the first time in many years Sarah felt her cheeks grow warm with embarrassment. 'Goodnight, Dr de Ville,' she muttered, angry with herself as she turned away and marched across the empty waiting-room.

'Goodnight Miss Courtney.'

His response had been polite, but Sarah could swear that she had detected a hint of amusement in his voice, and her cheeks were still heated as she entered the lift and jabbed the button for the ground floor.

Her colour subsided gradually to leave her pale once again, and she was clenching her teeth so fiercely that her jaw ached when she stepped out into the rain and walked across the well-lit car park outside the medical centre to where her godfather sat waiting behind the wheel of her dark green Mercedes.

'What's the verdict?' Ivor demanded anxiously when she got into the car beside him and slammed the door on the damp night air.

'He's prescribed something to help me sleep.' She produced the slip of paper from her handbag. 'I also have to be here at eight tomorrow morning for a series of tests which should take me through to lunchtime, and I shan't know the results until tomorrow evening.'

She flicked a drop of rainwater off the tip of her small, straight nose and stared directly ahead of her while she wrapped her arms about herself in an unconsciously protective gesture. She was angry, but most of all she was feeling unsure of herself, and that was something she had not experienced since those early days when she had been a novice at taking charge of a business such as Courtney's.

Ivor rested one arm on the steering-wheel as he turned in his seat to peer more closely at her rigid face. 'What did you think of Anton?'

Sarah raised her guard instinctively. She knew her godfather, and she knew only too well in which direction this seemingly innocent question might lead.

'He's thorough and leaves nothing to chance,' she answered him coolly.

'Are you speaking of him as a man, or as a doctor?'

'As a doctor, naturally.'

'Naturally,' he echoed drily, shifting his position behind the wheel and turning the key in the ignition. 'I'll stop off at a chemist to have that prescription filled before I take you home.'

Home was a luxury penthouse flat near the civic centre. Sarah sighed audibly half an hour later as she shed her raincoat in the hall and entered the spacious lounge where she kicked off her shoes. The carpeted floor felt good beneath her stockinged feet, and she sighed again. It was good to be home after a long, exhausting day. She had always been able to cope in the past, but just lately it had become a strain, and she dared not even begin to wonder at the reason why she had felt so ill since early morning.

She switched on the electric fire in the lounge. The October nights could still be considerably chilly, and there was an unfamiliar coldness inside her which she was beginning to think would never go away.

Ivor left her overnight bag in the hall and followed her into the lounge, his dark eyes narrowing with concern when he noticed her unnatural pallor and the frown creasing her smooth brow. 'You're not going to faint again, are you?'

'No.' She pressed her fingers briefly against her throbbing temples and grimaced. 'I'm just tired and I have a nagging headache.' Ivor accepted her statement in silence, then he turned towards the telephone on the marble-topped table against the wall. 'What are you doing?' she demanded as he lifted the receiver and punched out a number.

'I'm calling a taxi.' He glanced at her over his shoulder. 'You don't mind my using your phone, do you?'

'No, of course not, but I thought you might like to stay for a cup of coffee,' she explained hopefully, suddenly afraid at the thought of being left alone.

'You're tired, and so am I, my dear, so let's call it a day.' His smile warmed her, sweeping aside her ridiculous fears, and then he was speaking into the

telephone, requesting a taxi to be sent to Sarah's
address. 'I'll see to it that Lois cancels or postpones your
appointments for the morning, and I'd appreciate a call
from you when you arrive at the office,' he said when
he had replaced the receiver, and Sarah nodded as she
walked him to the door and opened it.

'Goodnight, Ivor.' She returned his fatherly kiss on
the cheek and added in a whisper, 'Thank you.'

'You don't have to thank me, Sarah,' he replied
smoothly, but there was a wicked gleam in the eyes that
met hers. 'I've always wanted you and Anton to meet,
but the opportunity never arose until now.'

'Oh, go away, you impossible man!' she instructed
with mock severity, but she could not suppress the
gurgle of husky laughter that rose in her throat as she
gave him a gentle push in the direction of the lift.

He waved as he walked away, and Sarah lingered in
the doorway until he was gone before she turned with a
sigh and went inside.

It was good to be home, she thought again, curling
her toes into the thick pile of the carpet as she glanced
about the room, which was comfortably and tastefully
furnished in pale green, cream and gold. The
cleaning-lady-cum-cook would have left a meal in the
refrigerator which Sarah could warm up within a few
seconds in the microwave oven, but she was not hungry.
She was too tired to eat, and the thought of a hot bath
before going to bed was far more appealing.

She collected her overnight bag in the hall and picked
up her discarded shoes. Her handbag lay on the chair
where she had flung it on her arrival, but her briefcase
was missing. It had stayed behind in her office when she
had been rushed off in such a hurry to see Dr de Ville.

The briefcase contained important documents which she had wanted to study at her leisure this evening, and not being able to do so was most annoying. There was nothing she could do about it now except shrug it off, and that was what she did as she picked up her things and marched through to her bedroom where she pulled the pins from her hair so that it tumbled in a wavy, brown-gold mass to her shoulders.

An hour later Sarah was lying curled up beneath the duvet on her queen-sized bed. She was listening to the muted sound of the traffic in the street below and staring at the glow of the city lights reflected against the wall of her darkened room. She had taken one of the tablets Dr de Ville had prescribed for her, and she was praying that it would work. She had not had a decent night's sleep in weeks, and she had a nasty feeling that the following day was going to present her with problems for which she would have to be in complete control of all her faculties.

'At the moment you're showing all the symptoms of stress,' Anton de Ville's words filtered into her mind.

Stress! Sarah scoffed mentally at the word. She had learnt to live with stress as her constant companion over the past six years. Why should if affect her in this way now? And, more to the point, what would the tests reveal?

'Oh, *damn!*' she muttered angrily, rolling over on to her other side and plumping up her pillow. 'That tablet isn't going to work!'

That was almost her last thought before the oblivion of sleep claimed her, and for the first time in several weeks it was the shrill ringing of the alarm clock that awakened her the following morning.

CHAPTER TWO

SARAH was not in a very good mood when she arrived at Dr Anton de Ville's rooms shortly after five-thirty that evening.

It had been a wet, bleak day from the start, and she had had to spend almost four gruelling hours at the medical centre that morning, allowing herself to be pricked and prodded and wired up to machines that bleeped ominously or had scratched out illegible data on to graphic paper. She had arrived back at the store shortly before lunch that day to find a pile of important correspondence on her desk which had needed her immediate attention, and the afternoon had been crammed with appointments to such an extent that she had barely had time to speak to her godfather.

Anton de Ville was standing beside his desk when Sister Jarvis ushered Sarah into the consulting-room. His one hand was thrust deep into the pocket of his white coat, and with the other he was flicking through the papers in what she presumed was her medical file. He turned, meeting Sarah's frosty gaze before his cursory glance flicked over her tall, slender frame in the stylish grey trousers and matching knee-length jacket of the finest wool, and his professional mask slipped for a fraction of a second to reveal a glimmer of appreciation.

'I was beginning to think you weren't coming,' he said, his mask intact once again as he waved her into a chair.

'I was held up in the traffic, she explained, her husky

23

voice clipped and cool as she seated herself.

'The tests were all negative,' he said when he saw her glance shift briefly to the opened file on his desk.

'Then I take it there's nothing wrong with me?'

'I didn't say that,' he deflated that swelling sensation of relief inside her, and confusion mingled with disbelief in the eyes she raised to his.

'But if the tests were negative, then surely——'

'When was the last time you took a break away from work to have a decent holiday?' he interrupted her with an unexpected harshness as he discarded her file and seated himself on the corner of the desk with his arms crossed over his broad chest. 'Two years ago? Three years, perhaps?' he persisted when Sarah remaind silent.

'What's that got to do with the way I've been feeling lately?' she demanded defensively.

'It has *everything* to do with it.' His probing, clinical glance lifted from her tightly clenched hands in her lap to her face, and Sarah was suddenly very much aware of the fact that there were lines of strain about her eyes and mouth which her carefully applied make-up had failed to conceal. 'It's become imperative that you take a complete break away from your work for a period of no less than six weeks,' he continued, 'and I would like to suggest that you don't waste time in making the necessary arrangements.'

'What you're suggesting is absolutely out of the question! I can't simply drop everything at a moment's notice and go away on an extended holiday. I have an extremely busy period ahead of me, and I——'

'I don't somehow think you've understood me very well, Miss Courtney.' Anton de Ville cut across Sarah's protestations this time with a note of urgency in his

authoritative voice as he rose to his feet and parted his
white coat to thrust his hands into the pockets of his grey
corded trousers. 'I'm going to give you a choice,' he
explained, frowning down at her. 'You could take that
six-week holiday *now*, or you could go on pushing
yourself beyond your limit and end up in a sanatorium
for a period of two to three months.'

'Are you telling me that—that I'm——' Sarah halted
and swallowed convulsively as an involuntary shiver
raced through her.

'In layman's terms, Miss Courtney, you've been
pushing yourself *too* hard for *too* many years, and
you're on the verge of a total collapse.'

He spoke knowledgeably as if he was in possession
of facts which she had not given him, and Sarah was
instantly on her guard. What information had her
godfather passed on to this man who happened to be the
son of an old friend? She felt her stomach turning in
much the same way as when she had been confronted
with a crisis at Courtney's in the past, but she rallied
swiftly. This was ridiculous! She was not going to allow
herself to be frightened into neglecting her
responsibilities and her commitments. The holiday
could wait, she decided, a wave of unreasonable anger
surging through her.

She rose without speaking, terminating this
consultation of her own accord, and Anton de Ville
made no attempt to detain her. He escorted her to the
door, and she paused there for a moment to look up into
his rugged face. 'Thank you for your time and your
trouble, Dr de Ville,' she said with rigid politeness.

'Don't take my advice lightly, Miss Courtney,' he
warned with a hint of mockery in his eyes, but his deep,

velvety voice remained grave. 'You need a long holiday, and you need it soon.'

Sarah left without responding to his statement. She would decide for herself whether or not she needed a holiday, and right now a holiday was way down on her list of obligations.

Her anger had deserted her when she arrived at her flat that evening, but she lapsed into an oddly pensive mood. She bathed and changed into a long-sleeved towelling robe before she sat down to the meal she had warmed in the microwave oven, but she did no more than peck at her food before she took her plate through to the kitchen to dispose of its contents. She returned to the lounge with a cup of filter coffee and, armed with several important documents which she had brought from the office, curled up comfortably on the high-backed chair in front of the electric fire, but her concentration was at a very low ebb.

'When was the last time you took a break away from work to have a decent holiday?'

Anton de Ville's query leapt unbidden into her mind, and this time it triggered the latch on the door to her past. She did not want to remember, the past was best forgotten, but she found that she was incapable of curbing the flow of her thoughts.

She had been fourteen when her father, Edmond Courtney, had opened his first store in a narrow side-street in Cape Town. With the valued assistance of a handful of people, working for love more than money during those early days, Courtney's began its slow, steady climb towards success. Edmond Courtney's main aim had been to provide exclusively designed clothes at a price which the average man and woman on the street could afford, and his dream had been that his business would grow until there was a Courtney's store in every major South African city. Five years later, with the much publicised opening of a Courtney's store in Johannesburg, Edmond Courtney's dream had been well on its way to becoming a reality.

Sarah had grown up lonely and unsure of herself. Her mother had died when she was eight, and at nineteen Sarah had still been making many futile attempts to get close to her autocratic father to, just once, win his approval. It was perhaps for this reason that she had not opposed her father's decision not to enrol her at a business college after she had left school.

'A woman's place is in the home,' he had insisted, and Sarah had accepted her fate resignedly. It had been important to her to please her father, and taking charge of their home and entertaining his guests had been a mammoth task, but even in this Edmond Courtney had succeeded in making her feel inadequate.

It was also at this time that Sarah met Nigel Kemp, a graduate from university who had been newly appointed to the staff at Courtney's in Cape Town.

Nigel!

Sarah drew a shuddering breath, and the sheaf of papers slid unheeded from her lap to the floor as she raised her cup to her lips with hands that shook and gulped down a mouthful of coffee. She did not want to remember beyond this point, the memories were becoming too painful, but her mind was like a vehicle which had careered into an uncontrolled skid.

Nigel Kemp was handsome and arrogant and, at twenty-nine, he had been ten years older than Sarah. He had also been ambitious, a quality which Edmond

Courtney had admired, and it had soon become common knowledge that Nigel was being primed for a key position at Courtney's, but his ambitions had gone far beyond that. He had seen himself as the man most likely to take over the business from Edmond Courtney, and Sarah had been the key to his success.

She had been too innocent and trusting at the time, and in too great a need for love and attention to guess the motive behind Nigel Kemp's sudden interest in her. She had always considered herself plain and unattractive, but with the shrewd use of charm and flattery Nigel had proceeded to make her feel like a desirable woman instead of the gauche, incompetent child she had believed she was. Edmond Courtney had thought very highly of him, and he had encouraged their courtship, but Sarah could not blame him for what had followed. Nigel had swept her off her feet, and for the first time in her life she had believed herself to be madly in love.

They were married less than two months after their first meeting, and Sarah had imagined herself to be the happiest woman on earth, but their marriage had been a disaster almost from the very beginning.

Sarah's humiliation was still as fresh in her mind as if she had just endured one of Nigel's contemptuous outbursts. She rose jerkily from her chair and walked to the window to grip the windowsill, her knuckles whitening as she stared blindly out across the city with its tall buildings and flickering lights. Her body felt cold and clammy and she was suddenly gasping for air like someone who had just emerged from a terrible nightmare, but her mind would not allow it to end there.

Two years later, at the age of twenty-one, she had

been caught up in yet another disaster. Edmond and Nigel had lost their lives when their yacht had been caught in a storm along the treacherous Cape coast.

It had been five weeks after their untimely deaths that Ivor Shaw had paid a visit to the Courtney residence. He had found Sarah wandering aimlessly through the spacious and picturesque gardens surrounding the rambling old house she had shared with her father and her husband, and that confrontation with her godfather had changed the course of her life.

She could sell, Ivor had informed her, or she could exercise her right as Edmond Courtney's daughter and take charge of Courtney's.

Sarah had not wanted to sell everything her father had worked so hard to achieve, and neither had she considered herself suitably equipped to step into her father's position, but her godfather had been very persuasive. 'It's time you got up off your butt and took charge of yourself as well as Courtney's. There's nothing to it,' he had added reassuringly. He would help her wherever he could if she was prepared to work hard and learn everything there was to know about the business, and that was exactly what Sarah had done.

Everything else, up to that point, could be considered a holiday in comparison. That was six years ago, and she had never had a holiday since.

Sarah sighed heavily as she turned away from the window to warm herself in front of the electric fire. She would never forget how Ivor had bullied her out of that shell into which she had withdrawn, and neither would she forget those first traumatic months at Courtney's.

She had started her education at the factory, speaking to everyone from the sewing-room up through to the

cutters and designers before going on to management
level. Not even the cleaners were left in peace. Sarah
had delved into records and had asked questions until
the staff must have felt like screaming whenever they
saw her coming. She had done the same at the store,
starting in the showroom before she eased her way up
into the administrative departments.

She had worked almost day and night, studying
business methods with a private tutor and sitting in on
meetings with her godfather temporarily in the chair. In
the process of learning she had also discovered
something about herself which she had not known
before. She had inherited her father's razor-sharp mind
and flair for business, and she had thanked God for that.

Sarah made her first major decision eight months
after taking charge of Courtney's. She sold the house in
Constantia, literally and figuratively closing the doors
on the past, and she left Cape Town to establish her
headquarters in Johannesburg, but she did not make this
transition on her own. Her godfather had been with
Courtney's from the very beginning, working on a
part-time basis as the firm's chief accountant and, like
Sarah, he had no family ties. When she offered Ivor a
permanent post with Courtney's as her financial and
personal adviser, he had accepted, and neither of them
had had cause to regret their decision.

The marble-faced clock on the mantelshelf chimed
the hour, startling Sarah out of her reverie. It was ten
o'clock. She crossed the room and bent down to pick up
the documents which lay scattered on the carpeted floor
beside her chair. The room suddenly started spinning
crazily, and she sat down quickly, her racing pulses
slowing down gradually to a dull, painful thudding in

her chest. An aching lameness surged into her limbs, leaving in its wake an odd feeling of exhaustion, and she closed her eyes for a moment as she leaned back in the chair.

She was forced to acknowledge the truth. She had perhaps pushed herself a little too hard for too many years, but her work had been her salvation, and she had willingly buried herself in it, shutting out everything else. She had driven herself without mercy, determined to make Edmond Courtney's dream a reality, and in six years she had succeeded. There was a Courtney's store in almost every major city in the country, and still there was that force inside her, driving her on in the search of new and greater conquests and achievements.

'Don't take my advice lightly,' Anton de Ville had warned. 'You need a long holiday, and you need it soon.'

Sarah grimaced as she returned the documents to her briefcase without reading them. This was an extremely awkward time for her to think of a holiday, she decided as she switched off the lights and went through to her bedroom.

'You could take that six-week holiday *now,* or you could go on pushing yourself beyond your limit and end up in a sanatorium for a period of two to three months.'

An involuntary shiver raced along her spine as she recalled Anton de Ville's warning. Perhaps she would be wise to give this matter more serious consideration. A six-week sojourn at a quiet resort sounded infinitely more appealing than an enforced stay in a sanatorium for a two to three month period.

Sarah was studying the month-end reports when the telephone system on her desk buzzed, and her glance slid automatically to her wristwatch. It was a quarter to five. Almost time to go home, she was thinking as she lifted the receiver tiredly and pressed the appropriate button on the control panel.

'Mr Shaw is here to see you, Miss Courtney,' Lois Beecham announced Ivor's return from Bloemfontein.

'Send him in, Lois.'

Sarah replaced the receiver and rose slowly from behind her desk. She felt unsteady on her feet, but she was becoming accustomed to that odd feeling of dizziness and weakness whenever she had been seated for a long time, and she was walking round her desk when her godfather entered her office and closed the door behind him.

'Hello, Ivor,' she smiled, kissing him on his leathery cheek and relieving him of the jacket he had draped over his arm before she walked towards the mahogany cabinet against the wall. 'Would you like a drink?'

Ivor smiled and nodded. 'A whisky would do nicely, thank you.'

'What's the news from the Bloemfontein branch?' she asked, dropping ice into a glass and adding whisky to it before she poured herself a glass of sherry.

'Business is progressing smoothly, and Steve de Vos will give you a full report first thing in the morning.' Sarah turned to hand him his drink, and the lines on his forehead deepened as he studied her pale, pinched face. 'You're looking rather ragged around the edges,' he said, swallowing down a mouthful of whisky.

'I've had rather a hectic day,' she laughed, trying to brush aside his remark as she seated herself beside him on the comfortable leather couch and sipped at her sherry.

'It's been more than two weeks since you went to see Anton, Sarah,' he reminded her gravely. 'When are you going to be sensible and take that holiday he suggested?'

'I can't simply drop everything and go off on a holiday!' she protested hotly, but deep down inside she was beginning to admit that she could recognise in herself the signs of someone who was close to cracking under pressure.

'You've proved yourself more capable than your father during these past six years, and it's about time you gave Steve the chance to prove *his* worth if you don't want to end up losing him to another company.'

Ivor had followed his compliment up with a warning which Sarah could not ignore. It was true, she thought as she watched her godfather swallow down another mouthful of whisky. She had not been entirely fair to Steve since he joined the firm, and she might lose him if she did not give him more responsibility.

'*Dammit*, Sarah!' Ivor exploded angrily, misinterpreting her silence. 'Why did you engage the services of a qualified assistant if you won't allow him to ease the burden on your shoulders?'

'I'll have a serious talk with Steve in the morning,' Sarah promised, making a snap decision, and almost laughed out loud at the look of incredulity that replaced the anger on her godfather's face. 'I don't suppose you could recommend a place where a tired body like myself would find peace and tranquillity for six weeks?' she asked, amusement lurking in her eyes as she crossed one long, shapely leg over the other and raised her glass of sherry to her lips.

'It just so happens that I've heard of a little place called Rosslee on the Natal south coast.' Ivor had rallied swiftly and he leaned towards her with a faintly mocking smile curving his mouth. 'I'm told it's an absolute haven for the weary,' he added, lowering his voice almost conspiratorially. 'And they guarantee the restoration of your soul or you get your money back.'

'It sounds like paradise,' she responded with a certain amount of scepticism.

'Anton assures me that it is.'

For no apparent reason Sarah felt her insides contract in a nervous spasm. 'You've discussed this with Dr de Ville, and he told you about Rosslee?'

'Your name did enter into the conversation the other day when we met by chance at the club, and he happened to mention that Rosslee was ideal for someone who needed to regain their strength and vitality.' Ivor offered this explanation while totally unaware of that strange tension he had aroused in Sarah. 'It appears Anton has been there a couple of times himself.'

'I see.' She took a sip of sherry and forced herself to relax. 'Well, if it's supposed to be such a marvellous place, then I might just consider going there.'

'I'm glad you're being sensible at last, my dear, and first thing in the morning I'll start making the necessary arrangements for you to leave as soon as possible.' Ivor drained his glass and rose purposefully to his feet. 'Speak to Steve about taking charge while you're away, and all you have to do after that is pack your bags.'

'Aren't you rushing things a bit?' she demanded protestingly as she got up and watched her godfather shrug his tall, bulky frame into his jacket.

'There's absolutely no sense in delaying matters, and I would prefer to think of you at Rosslee rather than as a patient in some dreadful sanatorium.' He kissed her on the cheek, his expression severe. 'You've earned this break, Sarah, and I can guarantee that Courtney's will still be here when you return!'

Rosslee was a small, secluded seaside resort situated a few kilometres south of Scottburgh. Besides the hotel there was a garage, a post office and a general dealer which sold almost everything from a safety-pin to an antique dresser. Below the hotel, along the rocky stretch of coastline, there were half a dozen privately owned chalets, and Sarah had to agree that, set among the indigenous trees and the lush sub-tropical vegetation of the Natal south coast, Rosslee *was* a veritable paradise for someone in search of a rest cure.

The sprawling, two-storeyed Rosslee Hotel with its natural terraced garden rated no more than two stars, but the residents were offered a wholesome nourishing meal three times a day, and Sarah's room on the upper floor was spacious and airy with a magnificent view of the Indian Ocean.

The hotel belonged to Walter and Angela Morgan, a charming couple in their early forties who also acted as caretakers for the owners of the chalets. They had welcomed Sarah on her arrival with a warmth and friendliness which had made her feel instantly at home, but privately Sarah had had grave doubts about coming to a place like Rosslee.

'This has to be a complete break with no form of communication to disrupt your holiday. You're to go to Rosslee and forget that such a place as Courtney's exists,' her godfather had instructed when he had seen her off at the airport.

'You're expecting the impossible, Ivor.'

'Promise you'll try.'

Sarah had promised, but that was before she had arrived at Rosslee. It was out of season, the hotel guests had dwindled to a mere handful, and the transition from her normally active life to this leisurely existence was so drastic that she wondered frantically how she was going to keep herself occupied during the weeks ahead of her.

The first few days had been the worst. She had sat and stared at the telephone on her bedside cupboard, thinking she would go mad if she did not call to find out what was happening at Courtney's during her absence, and at night she had lain awake until desperation drove her into the bathroom to take one of the sleeping tablets Dr de Ville had prescribed.

It was November, and soon it would be summer in southern Africa. The climate along the south coast was warm and temperate during the winter months as if summer had lingered on the doorstep, but during the summer months the heat and humidity could be discomfiting to someone who was unaccustomed to it.

Sarah also soon discovered that everything at the hotel seemed to be geared towards outdoor living and, weather permitting, morning and afternoon tea would be served out on the wide patio overlooking the swimming-pool area where colourful umbrellas shaded the tables, chairs and loungers which had been set out on the smooth lawn.

She was having afternoon tea out on the shaded patio towards the end of her first week at Rosslee when she realised that she was being subjected to the intensely curious observation of an elderly woman with snow-white hair which had been plaited and coiled into a strangely elegant band about her head. Sarah had grown accustomed to being stared at, but on this occasion she found it rather unsettling. She looked up, meeting that dark, searching glance, and for some obscure reason she felt compelled to acknowledge the woman's presence with a smile and a brief inclination of her head.

The woman rose at once as if Sarah's smile had triggered her into action and, bringing her cup of tea over to Sarah's table, she introduced herself.

'My name is Rose Poole,' she announced, and did not wait for an invitation to pull out a chair and to lower her frail body on to it. 'And I know who you are, of course,' she added before Sarah could formulate a response. 'You're Sarah Courtney, and last year you were the winner of the Businesswoman Of The Year award.'

Sarah felt a little stunned that Rose Poole should confront her with an achievement which a part of her would always feel unworthy of. 'You're obviously well informed,' she remarked with a wry smile.

'I read a lot since my husband passed away five years ago,' Rose Poole explained matter-of-factly. 'I get the daily newspapers, and I subscribe to several magazines which have, from time to time, featured articles about you.'

Sarah could recall vividly when necessity had forced her to grant those interviews, and even now she could feel herself tense inwardly at the memory of cameras clicking and flashbulbs which had almost blinded her while she had faced the barrage of questions the journalists had directed at her. If they could have bared her soul they would have done so, but they had failed to shatter her steely confidence, and her carefully erected barriers had remained intact to guard against the invasion of her privacy.

'Are you here at Rosslee on holiday?' Sarah questioned the older woman in a calculated attempt to steer the conversation away from herself.

'Oh, goodness me, no!' Rose Poole sipped at her tea and smiled self-consciously as she returned her cup to the saucer with a hand that had become unsteady with age. 'I'm a permanent resident here at the hotel,' she went on to explain. 'I have no children and no family to speak of, you see. That's why I decided to sell the house in Scottburgh and move in here after my husband died.'

Sarah felt a sharp twinge of compassion. Rose Poole was lonely, and Sarah knew that feeling.

'Forgive me for prying, Miss Courtney, but I've been watching you these past few days, and I've sensed that something is troubling you.' Rose Poole leaned towards Sarah with her arms crossed on the table in front of her, and Sarah could not escape the older woman's dark, probing glance which seemed to see beyond the solid wall of her reserve. 'Have you been ill?'

'In a manner of speaking,' Sarah evaded the query, reluctant to talk about herself, and most of all to someone she had only just met.

'Perhaps you've been working too hard.'

Working too hard. That phrase was beginning to sound like an accusation, and Sarah relented with a cynical smile. 'That's what my doctor says.'

'You couldn't have come to a better place than Rosslee for a rest cure, Miss Courtney,' the older woman assured her, the corners of her dark eyes creasing in a smile and her hands gesturing as if to encompass their picturesque surroundings. 'It may take a while for you to adapt to this leisurely life, but you'll soon begin to revel in it.'

'I hope you're right, Mrs Poole,' Sarah murmured with a great deal of scepticism.

'Call me Rose.'

Sarah hesitated a moment, then her soft mouth curved in an answering smile. 'Only if you'll call me Sarah.'

'You have beautiful hands, Sarah,' Rose remarked unexpectedly, reaching across the table to take Sarah's right hand between her own and turning it palm upwards. 'May I read your palm?'

Sarah understood Rose's query to be a joke and she reacted accordingly as she watched the older woman stare fixedly into her palm. 'I suppose you're going to tell me that there's a man lurking in my immediate future and that he's tall, dark and handsome.'

'You may laugh if you like, but I do see a man,' Rose replied with a gravity that wiped the faintly mocking smile off Sarah's face. 'I'm also loath to admit that he's tall and dark as you say. His face is a blur to me, but I have a strong suspicion that his features are striking rather than handsome.'

'Am I going to fall in love with him and live happily ever after?' Sarah demanded, her face suitably grave, but her husky voice was tinged with derisive mockery.

'That depends on whether you can shake off the past.' Sarah paled visibly, but Rose was too intent on studying her palm to notice. 'I can see that there's been much unhappiness, and there are still many shadows,' Rose continued. 'You've triumphed over some, Sarah, but there are others that go far deeper.'

Sarah felt the blood return to her cheeks in a rush that

made her temples throb when Rose Poole released her hand. Was this woman psychic, or was it simply a calculated guess which had steered her so close to the truth?

'I must go up to my room to shower and change into something decent before dinner,' Sarah excused herself, gesturing to the shorts and thin cotton top she was wearing as she rose hastily to her feet.

'I hope I haven't offended you with my observations?'

A worried frown creased Rose's brow, and Sarah could almost feel her agitation melt away as she looked down into that wrinkled face raised to hers. 'No offence was taken, Rose.' She smiled at her reassuringly. 'Perhaps you'd like to join me at my table this evening for dinner?'

Rose's face lit up with pleasure. 'Thank you, I'd like that very much.'

Sarah left the older woman out there on the patio and went inside. Rose's remarks were best forgotten, she decided as she crossed the hotel foyer with its chequered floor and potted palms. She had been taught at a very early age not to rely on predictions unless they were based on fact.

'Miss Courtney?' Sarah halted at the foot of the staircase and turned to see Angela Morgan walking towards her with an apologetic smile on her angular face. 'I couldn't help noticing that Rose Poole joined you for tea out on the terrace,' she said, coming straight to the point. 'I'd like to explain that, although Rose can be rather upsetting at times, she's really a kind old soul and quite harmless.'

'I'm sure she is,' Sarah replied with more

understanding than Angela Morgan was crediting her with.

'We've long ago dubbed her "Madame Rosa" because of this habit of hers to practice her palmistry on some of the hotel guests,' Angela explained unnecessarily. 'Humour her by all means, but don't take her ramblings too seriously, Miss Courtney.'

'I wouldn't take it too lightly either,' a masculine voice intervened, and Angela Morgan turned on her husband who had appeared on the scene as if from nowhere.

'Walter!' his wife exclaimed with a warning note in her voice, but he waved it away with an expressive gesture of his hand.

'You know as well as I do, Angela, that the old lady has been pretty accurate on quite a number of occasions.'

Angela bristled, preparing to do battle with him, but Sarah did not wait to hear more. She almost ran up the stairs to her room, and she was breathing so heavily when she closed the door behind her that she had to lean against it for a moment to steady herself.

Walter Morgan had rekindled Sarah's agitation. If Rose Poole had been accurate in her predictions on a number of occasions, then Sarah could only pray that this was not one of them. The shadows in her past were best left unexplored, and the last thing she wanted now, or in the future, was a man in her life.

CHAPTER THREE

THE day had been hot and humid, but a refreshing coolness had descended soon after sunset, and Sarah raised her face to the star-studded sky when she left the dining-room that evening and walked out on to the dimly lit patio. She drew the tangy sea air deep into her lungs and breathed out slowly again, trying to absorb the peace and tranquillity of her surroundings, but after two weeks at Rosslee she was still finding it difficult not to think about work.

Her growing friendship with Rose Poole helped considerably. They had shared the same table at mealtimes ever since that day when Sarah had invited Rose to join her for dinner, they had morning and afternoon tea together out on the patio, and sometimes they would sit down to a game of chess in the evenings before going to bed.

Sarah could not deny that she was missing Rose that evening. Rose had had to go to Scottburgh on business that afternoon, and she had not returned in time for dinner. She was a warm, generous woman who could occasionally say the most outrageous things, but Sarah never found her conversation boring.

A sigh escaped her, and she turned slightly at the sound of voices drifting towards her from the entrance of the hotel. A tall, dark-haired man in brown trousers and a white short-sleeved shirt was talking to Walter Morgan, and the light from the foyer was lengthening their shadows across the slate patio. There was something vaguely familiar about the wide-shouldered, lean-hipped frame of the man who stood with his back to Sarah, and she was still trying to place him when he turned suddenly so that his face was clearly visible in the light spiling out of the foyer.

Sarah's breath locked in her throat as she recognised the rugged features of Dr Anton de Ville. A million thoughts raced through her mind, and mingling with them was the intense desire to escape his notice. She backed a pace away, wanting to shrink into the shadows, but his glance collided with hers at that moment, and she stood as if turned to stone when she saw him take his leave of Walter Morgan and walk slowly towards her.

'Miss Courtney?' There was a measure of uncertainty in his deep, velvety voice, and Sarah was glad she had managed to control herself sufficiently to acknowledge his presence with a polite but rigid smile. 'This is a surprise!' he announced pleasantly when he stood no more than a pace away from her. 'You're the last person I expected to see here at Rosslee, but I'm glad to know you took my advice.'

'It sounded more like an ultimatum,' she responded accusingly, wishing she could see his face and not merely the outline of his head with the neatly trimmed dark hair that had a tendency to curl on to his forehead, but he was standing with his back to the dining-room light spilling out on to the patio, putting her at a disadvantage.

'I imagine it did sound like an ultimatum,' he conceded, 'but you'll agree that the gravity of your circumstances demanded it.'

'That's something I still have to discover for myself,'

she replied coldly, resenting that hint of laughter she had detected in his voice.

'I have no doubt you will, Miss Courtney,' he parried her statement calmly. 'Goodnight.'

What was Anton de Ville doing here at Rosslee? Sarah's racing heart slowly began to resume its normal pace as she watched him walk away from her across the patio with those long, easy strides which one attributed to an athlete.

'I told you there was a man in your future, and Anton de Ville seems to fit my description perfectly.'

Rose's voice had intruded unexpectedly on Sarah's disquieting thoughts, and she spun round jerkily to see the older woman emerging from the deep shadows of the crimson bougainvillaea ranking along the trellised section of the patio.

'Do you know Dr de Ville?'

'Everyone here at Rosslee knows him,' Rose informed Sarah with an expressive wave of her hands. 'He owns the chalet at the furthest end of the beach, and he comes here whenever he can get away from his busy life in Johannesburg.'

'I see.' An ugly suspicion was manifesting itself in Sarah's mind, and it made her wonder whether her godfather had been aware of the fact that Anton de Ville owned a chalet here at Rosslee when he had persuaded her to consider this seaside resort as the best place for a holiday.

'I gather Anton de Ville is the doctor who ordered you to take a holiday?' Rose questioned her, and Sarah pulled herself together with an effort.

'That's correct.'

Rose dragged her thin, silky shawl more closely

about her shoulders. 'You'll be seeing him again,' she stated confidently.

'I shall do my best *not* to see him again.'

'One word of warning, though,' Rose continued as if Sarah had not spoken. 'Anton de Ville is not a man who'll succumb easily to the idea of marriage.'

Sarah shivered as the cool breeze whipped playfully through the short hair at the nape of her neck which always seemed to escape from the combs holding her chignon in place, but the coolness of the night air had nothing to do with that icy feeling gripping her insides.

'I'm not looking for a husband!' she declared stonily, rejection coiling along every fibre of her being, but Rose was smiling at her with the tolerance of someone who believed she knew better.

'If you're not looking for a husband, then there's nothing to stop you enjoying his company.'

'You're taking a lot for granted, Rose.'

'I have a feeling about certain things.' Rose linked her arm through Sarah's as they went inside. 'Shall we play a game of chess?'

Sarah agreed, but she doubted whether she would be able to give the game her complete attention that evening. Anton de Ville's presence here at Rosslee had come as something of a shock, and Rose's presumptuous statement had succeeded in arousing an illogical stab of panic.

She had nothing to fear, Sarah reminded herself. She had realised long ago that she was emotionally and physically immune to men. They could never touch her again . . . never hurt her in the way she had been hurt before.

'You're worthless as a woman, Sarah! You're of no

use to me, or to any other man! Having you for a wife
might still have its financial compensations, but no man
in his right mind wants to take a cold slab to bed with
him!'

Nigel's cruel, humiliating accusation rose from the
ashes of her past. It had cut deep; too deep for her to
want to seek a repetition of that nightmare existence she
had led for two years, and taking charge of Courtney's
had been a much-needed antidote. She *was* immune.
Her relationships with men were now strictly confined
to business, she had made that absolutely clear over the
years, and that was how she intended it to stay.

Sarah lay stretched out on a lounger beside the deserted
pool, and her slender, bikini-clad body was gleaming
with the protective lotion she had applied to herself
before she had exposed herself to the stinging rays of
the afternoon sun. She had intended also to read the
mystery novel she had borrowed from the hotel library,
but it had failed to grip her attention after the third page,
and she had put it aside long ago.

The heat of the sun had injected her with an
unfamiliar but pleasant laziness, and she had closed her
eyes eventually to listen to the birdsong in the trees
soaring out above the ceaseless sound of waves rushing
towards the shore.

A shadow shifted across her face some minutes later.
She thought it was the steward who had come to collect
the glass which had contained the fruit juice she had
ordered earlier, but the next instant she heard the
intensely disturbing sound of Anton de Ville's familiar
voice saying, 'Good afternoon, Miss Courtney.'

Sarah murmured something in response, her lashes

lifting to reveal the displeasure in her tawny eyes, but it was not annoyance that made her heart skip an uncomfortable beat when she looked up into the smiling face of the man who was standing no more than a pace away from her with his strong, long-fingered hands resting in an arrogant stance on his lean hips.

Last night, when they had met on the patio, Sarah had had no difficulty in associating him with the sober, white-coated medical man she had had to consult some weeks ago in Johannesburg, but that was not how she was seeing him now.

His blue T-shirt clung to his broad, muscular chest like a second skin, but the white shorts hugging his hips drew her attention to his long, sun-browned legs, and her gaze lingered for a moment on muscled thighs and calves before she raised her glance with a self-conscious start. He was a man who pursued outdoor activities in his free time, his tanned, rugged features had told her that some time ago, but she had not known that the sunlight could set fire to the dark hair which persisted in falling across his broad forehead.

Sarah could not recall ever looking at a man in such detail, but neither could she recall ever meeting a man who had this power to stir her interest to such an extent, and it left her feeling strangely vulnerable.

'Rose told me I'd find you here,' he said, his blue gaze shifting over her briefly and taking in her appearance from the golden sheen of her shoulder-length auburn hair down to her shell-pink toenails, and his smile was approving when his eyes met hers again. 'You've acquired a nice tan.'

'Did you want to see me about something?' she asked coolly, sliding her sunglasses down on to the bridge of her nose, and she saw his smile deepen, making her unnervingly aware of the fact that her attempt to hide her embarrassment had gone unnoticed.

'I spent the morning trying to recover after yesterday's long car journey from Johannesburg, but I couldn't let the day pass without coming to enquire into my patient's progress,' he said, his chest and arm muscles rippling as he pulled up a chair and seated himself close to the lounger.

'Your patient is progressing very nicely, thank you,' she informed him in a voice that sounded horribly prim.

'I can see that.' His laugh was pleasantly throaty, his strong teeth flashing white against his tanned complexion, and, for the second time within a space of weeks, an embarrassing warmth stole into Sarah's cheeks.

She would not have donned her bikini if she had not believed that she would have the pool to herself that afternoon, and she was suddenly acutely conscious of the fact that she was wearing no more than two ineffectual scraps of material. The bikini was the latest and the most fashionable in the Courtney's swimwear division, it had been designed to cover the most essential parts of a woman's anatomy, but Anton de Ville was succeeding in making her feel naked as his blue gaze took a second trip along her slender frame stretched out on the lounger.

Her nerve-ends quivered in something close to alarm when his glance lingered for an unnecessary length of time on her small, firm breasts, but she could not even begin to explain the melting warmth invading the lower half of her body when his glance shifted down along her taut, flat abdomen, and her long, shapely legs.

If he had wanted to shock her into the discovery that he was a normal, virile male and not a dehumanised medical practitioner, then he was succeeding. His glance was blatantly sensual instead of clinical and impersonal while he carried out his inspection of her body, and the wave of heat that was now surging through her had nothing to do with the stinging warmth of the sun against her skin when she sat up with a jerk to put on her beach robe.

He observed her in silence while she thrust her arms into the short sleeves of her towelling robe and wrapped the garment around her. Sarah suspected that he was aware of her confusion and anger, and the tightening of his sensuous mouth confirmed it. 'What made you decide to come to a place like Rosslee?' he asked abruptly.

'I believe you told Ivor about Rosslee, and he passed on the rave reviews to me,' she answered him in a voice as clipped as his own while she fastened the belt of her robe about her slim waist and gave it an extra tug for firmness.

'Ah, yes, I remember now.' His clinical mask was once again firmly in place. It clashed with his casual attire, but it helped Sarah to clarify the situation between them while she watched him lean back in his chair and stretch his long, muscular legs out in front of him.

There was something she had to know. It had persisted in keeping her awake half the night, and it had plagued her for the best part of the day.

'Rose happened to witness our brief meeting out on the patio last night,' she began, observing Anton de Ville closely from behind the protective shield of her sunglasses, and there was an odd fluttering at the pit of her stomach when he directed a questioning glance at her. 'She told me afterwards that you own one of the chalets down on the beachfront, and I wondered . . .' Her husky voice faltered with embarrassment, but she regained control almost instantly. 'Was my godfather aware of this? Did he know that you intended coming here to Rosslee at this particular time of the year?'

'I never mentioned to Ivor that I'd bought a chalet here at Rosslee, and at the time of our meeting I had no idea when I'd be able to get away for a holiday.' He spoke convincingly, his glance not wavering from hers, and Sarah felt the tension ease out of her body as she saw his brow clear with understanding. 'I take it your godfather is in the habit of wanting to match you up with someone?'

Sarah nodded and looked away, her hair falling forward over her shoulders to hide the flush of embarrassment on her cheeks while her sunglasses veiled those ridiculous tears which relief had brought to her eyes.

'Just lately I've had that suspicion,' she confessed, the husky quality in her voice accentuated in the face of her emotional dilemma. 'And it makes me feel awkward.'

'I know what you mean.'

Yes, I'm sure you do, she thought in response to his grave reply.

This man was long past the youthful age. At their first meeting she had noticed a smattering of grey in the dark hair against the temples of this man with the ruggedly handsome appearance, and she was convinced that he could not have gone through life without a few well-meaning friends and members of the family arranging meetings with women in the hope of urging him into marriage.

'How long have you been here at Rosslee?' he asked, his deep, smooth voice adopting that professional tone which could have had Sarah believing they were back in his consulting room if it were not for their exotic sub-tropical surroundings.

Anton de Ville exuded a powerful aura of masculinity. It was leashed, but it was there, and Sarah might not have been aware of it before but she felt the pull of it now like a metal object might feel the tug of a magnet. It made her intensely curious, but she also sensed that it held an element of danger for her.

'I arrived two weeks ago,' she answered his query while she focused her attention on a bee investigating the glass in which she had had a soft drink earlier. 'I was met at Durban's Louis Botha airport and driven down to Rosslee because my godfather didn't trust me with a hired car. He said it might tempt me to cut my holiday short.'

His mouth quirked with a suggestion of a smile as if he might also not have trusted her in this instance. 'How do you feel?'

'I'm not sure,' she shrugged, in complete control of herself now as she swung her legs off the lounger to sit facing him. 'I've been finding it extremely difficult to divest myself of something which has become such a vital part of my existence over the years, and I find I can't sleep at night unless I take one of those tablets you prescribed for me.'

'It's very important that you get enough sleep, it's the best therapy anyone can prescribe for you, and I strongly advise you to take a tablet every night until you're absolutely sure you can do without it.'

His authoritative consulting-room manner was ridiculously displaced beside the hotel pool, and Sarah's innate sense of humour rose to the fore, lifting the corners of her generous mouth in a faintly mocking smile. 'This is an odd place for a consultation with one's doctor, isn't it?'

'You didn't consult *me*, I consulted *you*, but I would really prefer you to believe that I'm here as a friend and not as your doctor.' He looked up from his idle study of the canvas shoes on his feet, and his stern features relaxed into a disarming smile. 'Do you think we could be friends, Sarah?'

Her name sounded strange on his lips, so silky and smooth, and a curious sensation spiralled through her that left her feeling oddly weak at the knees. Could they be friends? No, *never*! She did not need to be clairvoyant to know that Anton de Ville was not a man who would be satisfied for any length of time with a platonic relationship, and that was all she would ever have to give a man.

'I've been told it isn't wise to become too friendly with one's doctor,' she deliberately evaded his query.

'Why is that, I wonder?' he demanded, his glance resting on the pulse at the base of her throat that conveyed her distress.

'Perhaps it's because patients are inclined to reveal too many secrets to their doctors, and that might make it awkward for them to indulge later in a normal relationship.'

'If that's so, then you have nothing to fear.'

'You mean our doctor/patient relationship has been too brief for me to reveal any of my innermost secrets to you?'

Her mocking rejoinder to his reassuring statement met with a reproving smile. 'If you have secrets, Sarah Courtney, then you're not the kind of woman who would divulge them to anyone unless you felt driven to it.'

It startled her that he could have summed her up so accurately after so short an acquaintance. But why, she wondered long after he had gone, had it felt as if she had been severely rebuked?

The answer eluded her, and she was still feeling uneasy about it when she went indoors half an hour later to shower and make herself presentable before dinner.

'I told you you'd see him again,' Rose remarked unexpectedly when they were halfway through their meal that evening, and Sarah's disturbed state of mind did not prevent her from knowing at once that Rose was referring to Anton de Ville.

'Rose?' she began warily, lowering her knife and fork and meeting the older woman's dark glance across the table with its centre arrangement of yellow chrysanthemums. 'No more predictions . . . not for me . . . please?'

'Don't tell me you're afraid of what Madame Rosa might have to tell you?'

'You know? About being called Madame Rosa, I mean?' Sarah asked in surprise, and a few curious glances were directed at their table when Rose threw back her snow-white head and laughed heartily.

'I'm well aware of the fact that Walter and Angela Morgan call me Madame Rosa behind my back, but I don't let it bother me,' she assured Sarah when she finally managed to control herself. 'And I promise—no more predictions. Not for you, Sarah.'

Anton de Ville's name was not mentioned again during the remainder of their meal, but for some obscure reason Sarah could still not get him out of her mind. Rose suggested a game of chess after dinner, but she declined on this occasion with the excuse that she wanted to have an early night, and Rose did not insist.

Sleep was, however, an elusive element. It had been that way for longer than Sarah cared to remember, but sleep was not what she was seeking on that particular evening—and at that early hour. A minor incident was beginning to assume the proportions of a major catastrophe in her mind, and she knew she had to deal with it swiftly and decisively.

Anton de Ville had made a tentative offer of friendship that afternoon and, in a very indirect way, she had rejected him. In the past she had dealt with similar offers in a much harsher manner without a twinge of conscience. Why then should her rejection of Anton de Ville's friendship leave her so disturbed?

Sarah kicked off her shoes beside the bed and crossed the carpeted floor on stockinged feet. She drew aside the heavy brocade curtains and filled her lungs with the tangy night air that filtered into her room through the open window.

The trees obscured her view of the beach with its natural pool among the rocks where families gathered for a swim free of the fear of sharks, but the Indian Ocean lay stretched out before her in the moonlight, and she could hear the waves breaking on the shore. A fleecy cloud drifted across the moon, dimming its brilliance and casting a shadow across the earth.

'There are still many shadows,' Rose had said that

afternoon when she had stared into Sarah's palm. 'You've triumphed over some, but there are others that go far deeper.'

Her life had once been filled with shadows. She had, as Rose had said, rid herself of most of them, but one shadow in particular had remained to dim the brilliance of her world. She could not share her secret shadow with anyone, and that justified her refection of Anton de Ville's friendship. He would not be satisfied with half-truths, he was a man who would demand to know everything, and she would rather die than suffer again the humiliation she had suffered at Nigel's hands.

Sarah was awake before dawn. She had always been an early riser—that was something these two weeks at Rosslee had not rid her of—and soon after her arrival she had begun the ritual of going for a walk along the beach to watch the sunrise before she returned to the hotel for breakfast.

She zipped herself into her khaki trousers and tucked her amber-coloured blouse into them with a haste that made her look dishevelled. She was impatient to escape the confining walls of her room, but a quick glance in the dressing-table mirror made her reach for her hairbrush. She pulled it through her hair with a few vigorous strokes and, leaving her hair free of its confining combs, she went downstairs quietly and left the hotel through the side entrance.

The air smelled fresh and clean, and she could hear the birds starting to stir in the trees when she walked along the narrow path that led down to the beach. This was the best part of the day, she decided as she paused at the bottom of the pathway to take off her low-heeled sandals, and she was smiling to herself when she stepped down on to the loose sand to begin her walk along the beach.

Ghost crabs darted for cover as she approached, moving swiftly in various directions like pale shadows flitting across the sand, but Sarah barely noticed them. She was staring out to sea, watching the waves which were like strips of turbulent froth, rolling towards the shore to batter the rugged rocks with a force that would send a foamy explosion of water shooting high into the air.

She felt the spray of water on her face, and the familiar taste of salt was on her lips when she explored it with the tip of her tongue. The sand was cool and damp beneath her bare feet, and the breeze was playing havoc with her hair, but she was only vaguely aware of these things as she paused to stare out across the restless expanse of water. She had always loved the sea, but circumstances had also caused her to fear it when she realised that the sea could relinquish its treasures to you as easily as it could take from you what you might cherish most.

Mist clouds hung low on the horizon that morning, jealously guarding the birth of a new day, and they seemed to disperse grudgingly when the sun finally commenced its slow, majestic rise into the sky. It bathed the earth in that pale glow of dawn, and Sarah expelled the air from her lungs on an ecstatic sigh at the beauty of it.

She was smiling when she turned to continue her walk, but her smile faltered and she stopped short as she saw Anton de Ville's tall, denim-clad figure walking bare-footed towards her along the beach from the direction of the chalets nestling among the trees.

His loose-limbed, athletic stride suggested a strength and stamina which she imagined he must need in his profession as much as she needed it in hers, but strength and stamina were two qualities which she seemed to lack at that moment when he walked up to her with that disarming smile creasing his rugged, clean-shaven features.

'Good morning, Sarah.'

'Good morning, Dr de Ville,' she heard herself respond on a breathless note which belonged to someone who had just completed an energetic sprint rather than to her, but she rapidly regained her composure despite that hint of mockery she thought she had detected in his eyes.

'We're a long way from my consulting-room, Sarah,' he pointed out with an unfamiliar flash of anger in his eyes. 'Call me Anton.'

'As you wish . . . Anton,' she responded obligingly in a cool, controlled voice which was beginning to sound more like herself.

The sea breeze had whipped a natural colour into her cheeks, and her tawny eyes sparkled mysteriously like jewels in the morning light, but she was unaware of this as she found herself subjected to his intent appraisal.

'I didn't expect to find you out here on the beach at this early hour of the morning,' he said at length, his glance lingering with interest on her tall, slender figure, and Sarah would have been appalled rather than pleased to discover that her windswept appearance had a sexual appeal that few men could ignore.

'After six years in Johannesburg I'd almost forgotten how beautiful it is to watch the sun rise into a sky that isn't filled with city smog,' she explained, and Anton nodded with understanding as he directed his gaze out across the ocean.

'This is one of the things I miss most when I have to return to the city after a spell here at Rosslee.'

Sarah studied his strong profile unobtrusively, her glance tracing the broad forehead, the high-bridged nose which showed signs of having been broken at some stage, the sensuous curve of his often stern mouth, and the square, jutting jaw. She could remember thinking at their first meeting that he was not the best-looking man she had ever seen, but his face had character, it mirrored his strength and reliability, and that was what she found so attractive.

Take care, Sarah Courtney! she warned herself severely. Just because you find this man attractive it doesn't mean you're any different from the sexually inadequate woman who was once married to Nigel Kemp!

'How long are you staying?' she asked, allowing her glance to linger for a moment longer on that rugged profile before she looked away.

'Three weeks,' he said, turning to her with his fingers pushed into the hip pockets of his tight-fitting denims. 'I usually prefer to take my leave during the winter months to escape the cold weather up on the reef, but that isn't always possible.'

'What happens to your patients when you're away on holiday?'

'I have arrangements with a colleague of mine at the medical centre. I take care of his patients when he's away, and he very kindly does the same for me.'

'Don't your patients object to having to see someone

else when you're away?' she asked curiously, thinking she would not find it so easy to consult a doctor who had taken the place of the one she had become accustomed to.

'I think my patients trust me enough to know that I wouldn't refer them to someone whom I didn't have faith in myself.'

Sarah had no cause to dispute that statement. Patients had to have faith in their doctors, that was perhaps the most important part of the healing process, and she somehow knew instinctively that Anton de Ville was someone who could be trusted implicitly as a man and as a doctor.

There was a strange stirring in her breast, an awakening perhaps, but she did not question it as she followed his gaze to where the sun had risen to its full glory on the distant horizon. It blinded her, and she looked away, focusing her attention instead on the restless mass of water which stretched as far as the eye could see. The sea had always fascinated her, but more so now as unwanted memories crowded her mind.

'The ocean has a temperament of its own,' she voiced her thoughts without actually intending to. 'It can be calm and tranquil one minute, and wild and tempestuous the next.'

Anton turned to look at her with a flicker of unexpected understanding in his eyes as if he had sensed the tragedy which had prompted her remark. 'Do you have time for a cup of coffee before you return to the hotel?' he asked as he saw her glance at the slim gold watch strapped to her wrist.

Sarah's instinctive reaction was to decline his invitation, but she hesitated. She had rejected his offer of friendship the day before, and her conscience still troubled her because of it. There was no harm in accepting his friendly invitation. Was there?

'A cup of coffee would be nice, thank you,' she agreed before that nagging little voice at the back of her mind could make her voice her customary refusal.

CHAPTER FOUR

ANTON DE VILLE'S chalet vaguely resembled the chalets at the skiing resorts in the Swiss Alps. It was perhaps the carved wooden railings around the balcony on the upper floor that gave Sarah that impression, but that was where the similarity ended. The outside walls had been built with decorative bricks, and the windowpanes were set in durable aluminium frames which would neither rust nor swell in the weather conditions along the coast

The ceiling in the roomy lounge was of an attractive pine, and so was the carved balustrade on the staircase leading to the upper floor. The wall-to-wall carpeting was a flecked, serviceable brown, while the sofa and armchairs were comfortably padded and upholstered in a rich cream material, and the curtains at the windows were a deep gold.

Sarah glanced about her, searching for personal mementoes which might give her an insight into Anton's character, but there was nothing to adorn the room except two landscape paintings by an artist she did not know. The chalet was a holiday home and no more, she realised with a certain amount of disappointment.

Anton's blue, smiling glance captured hers, and he raised his arms in a sweeping gesture. 'What do you think?'

'It looks like a place one could relax in.' She meant that sincerely as she cast yet another brief glance about her. 'Did you choose the décor?'

'The décor more or less came with the chalet.' He indicated the sliding glass doors. 'The patio is through there.'

Sarah preceded him out on to the patio which was sheltered by the indigenous trees which had been left undisturbed by conservation-conscious builders when the chalet had been erected, and her low-heeled sandals made a dull tapping sound on the reddish-brown Italian tiles when she walked towards the carved wooden railings surrounding the patio.

'You have an unobstructed view of the sea from here,' she heard herself remarking for want of anything better to say. She could feel Anton's eyes resting on her intently, and it unnerved her for some reason.

'Make yourself comfortable while I get the coffee, Sarah,' he suggested without commenting on her remark. 'Do you take milk and sugar?'

'Milk, but no sugar, thank you,' she said, turning, and his glance held hers briefly but compellingly before he went inside.

Why am I nervous? she wondered as she lowered herself on to one of the white-painted wrought-iron chairs that matched the circular table out on the patio. Anton de Ville was no different from any other man she had met in the past, so why was she beginning to feel nervous in his company?

Sarah knew the answer to her own queries. Her meetings with other men had occurred in public places, but this was the first time in years that she had been actually alone with a man, in his home, and for reasons other than business.

What was she afraid of? Was she afraid that he might

pounce on her and so discover her terrible secret? No, Anton had not given her the impression that he was the type of man who would pounce on a woman. Besides, Sarah reasoned with herself, he was her doctor and his interest in her was purely from a medical point of view.

A cynical voice at the back of her mind told her that the latter was not quite true, but she chose to ignore it for the moment, and when she looked up she saw Anton emerge from the chalet with a cup of steaming coffee in each hand.

He was a good conversationalist, Sarah discovered while they were drinking their coffee, and she slowly began to relax. Being alone with him was not the nerve-racking experience she had imagined it might be.

'What made you take back your maiden name after your husband and your father were killed in that yachting accident?' They had been discussing the beauty of Rosslee's off-the-map existence when Anton leapt in with that query, and Sarah was caught totally off her guard.

Where had he got that information?

'You're a very successful businesswoman, and that makes you newsworthy.' His eyes mocked her as he answered her unspoken query. 'And my choice of reading matter does happen to extend beyond the medical journals,' he added, making her feel as if she had been rapped over the knuckles once again.

'I legally took back the name Courtney to avoid unnecessary confusion when I took over my father's business.' That was not the only reason, but he need not know that she had changed her name in a deliberate attempt to put the pain-filled past behind her and make a new beginning.

'It must have been a traumatic experience for you,

losing your father and your husband at the same time.'

Her expression became shuttered and she looked away. 'Yes, it was,' she said at length when she had her voice under control.

'You don't want to talk about it, do you?'

His perception was uncanny. He seemed to know her thoughts and her feelings as if he had tuned himself in on to her wavelength, and it was more than a little frightening.

'No, I don't want to talk about it,' she admitted, placing her empty cup on the table and forcing her lips into a semblance of a smile. 'Tell me about yourself instead.'

'What do you want to know?'

Sarah gestured vaguely and rather nervously with her hands. 'Whatever you feel like telling me.'

'Well, let's see . . .' His narrowed gaze went out across the ocean that lay shimmering in the morning sunlight, and his smile was faintly derisive as he leaned back in his chair and stretched his long legs out in front of him. 'I was born in Cape Town thirty-eight years ago. I was seven years old when my father divorced my mother and moved up to Johannesburg, and I spent my childhood being shuttled back and forth between my parents until I was old enough to make up my own mind about where I wanted to live and what I wanted to do with my life. My father passed away a couple of years ago, but my mother is still alive and living, not so happily, I believe, with her third husband in Cape Town.' His mocking glance captured hers and held it effortlessly. 'Anything else you want to know?'

He had nice eyes, Sarah realised not for the first time. they were so incredibly blue, and they were smiling, but there was remembered pain there as well. Oh, yes—the pain. She had had to endure her own fair share of pain in the past, and something inside her seemed to reach out to him in a way it had never done with anyone else before.

'I think I can understand why you're not the marrying kind.' Sarah had voiced her thoughts softly, unintentionally, but his surprised expression made her smile. 'Rose told me,' she explained, and he laughed derisively.

'I wouldn't say I'm not the marrying kind. God knows, I've come close to it a few times over the years, but something has always held me back,' he confessed without rancour. 'I feel it's important that I make the right choice, and if I ever take a wife it will have to be because I'm absolutely sure I could spend the rest of my life with her.' Anton drew his feet up beneath his chair and leaned towards her across the table. 'Wasn't that how you felt when you married Nigel Kemp?'

Sarah became aware of a suffocating pressure in her chest. The topic of conversation had bounced back to her with the speed of a ball in a squash court, but she felt like someone who had been caught without a racket.

'I was barely nineteen when I married Nigel,' she said coldly, getting up and walking away from him towards the wooden railings. 'I was awkward, unsure of myself and very plain, and I was flattered that a man as good-looking as Nigel could be interested in me. My father's approval seemed to seal my fate, and I grew to believe that I loved Nigel enough to marry him.'

'I gather you soon discovered your mistake?'

'Yes.'

Oh, yes! She had discovered her mistake all too soon, she thought cynically as she gripped the railings in front of her. She might have loved Nigel, she might even have been happy to spend the rest of her life with him, but fate had stepped in to change her body into something which would be of no use to any man, and, whatever her feelings had been for Nigel, they had no longer existed after the first four months of their marriage.

'I can't imagine the celebrated Sarah Courtney as someone who was ever awkward and unsure of herself, and you're most certainly not plain,' Anton referred to her earlier statement, his chair scraping on the tiles and catching her nerves on the raw as he rose to his feet to join her at the rails.

'You didn't know me when I was nineteen.' Her tawny eyes clouded and a cynical smile hovered about her mouth as she remembered the gangling, vulnerable girl she had been. She had known so little about life when she married Nigel, and she had known even less about fashion two years later when she had had the temerity to step into her father's shoes. 'Taking over Courtney's has helped me to grow and develop over the years as a person in my own right, and what I have now is something I shan't give up without a fight.'

'Your business life is always very much in the news, but what about the private side to Sarah Courtney?' Anton leaned towards her, his hand sliding along the rail until it rested close to hers. 'Is there a man tucked away somewhere that no one has been told about, Sarah?'

His nearness was flinging her into confusion, making her intensely aware of every inch of his long-limbed, muscular body, and she resorted to anger as the most natural form of defence against the alien forces he was arousing inside her.

'I don't have time for personal relationships,' she said

icily, her eyes sparking yellow-brown fire. 'My business and private life have become one.'

'That doesn't sound to me like a very healthy situation,' he mocked her, and Sarah's anger rose by several degrees.

'It may not sound healthy to you, but I happen to enjoy my life the way it is. I work long hours, but I find my job stimulating and exciting.'

'And time-consuming.'

'That too,' she agreed coldly.

'I don't suppose you're ever lonely.' His rugged face was an unfathomable mask, but his voice once again seemed to rebuke her. 'You've painted such a self-sufficient picture of yourself, Sarah Courtney, that I don't suppose you ever experience a moment in your life when you feel the need to reach out and find someone there for you.'

His big hand had shifted over hers on the rail, his fingers gently stroking the delicate network of veins against the inside of her wrist, and the sensations his touch aroused were like a tingling current of electricity trailing up along her arm and down her spine.

'I am lonely . . . sometimes,' she heard herself confessing while she tried desperately to control the odd tremors gripping her insides.

'How do you deal with it?'

Better than I'm dealing with this, she thought weakly as she stared down at the sheen of fine dark hair against the back of his sun-browned hand.

'I find something with which to keep myself occupied until the feeling passes,' she said, angry with herself rather than with Anton as she freed her hand from his and turned towards the sliding glass doors that led inside. 'I have to go.'

'Sarah!' Anton had moved swiftly, his bare feet silent on the tiled floor which was bathed in dappled sunlight as he gripped her arm to detain her at the door. 'There is a life beyond Courtney's, Sarah,' he warned harshly, his fingers biting into the soft flesh above her elbow. 'Don't shut it out.'

Sarah was of average height, at five foot six she had been described by some as tall, but she had to tilt her head by several degrees to subject Anton to the chilling anger of her glance.

'How I choose to live my life is no concern of yours, and when I want your advice I'll ask for it!' She jerked her arm free of his disturbing clasp and spun away from him. 'Thanks for the coffee, and don't bother to see me to the door!'

Sarah left him standing there on the patio as she stormed out of the chalet, but her anger had subsided to leave her exhausted and more than a little ashamed of herself when she finally reached the seclusion of her room at the hotel. Anton had been concerned for her, she recognised that fact now, and she had repaid him with rudeness.

She could not understand what had possessed her to behave like that. His probing questions had angered her, but she had been asked those questions many times before without losing her control.

Fear! Her actions had been motivated by fear! She realised this with a start when she had stripped off her clothes to step beneath the cool jet of water in the shower cubicle.

'That's ridiculous!' she laughed out loud at herself, but her quick, assessing mind was already sifting

through the facts in its search for clarification.

There was something about Anton de Ville that set him apart from any other man she had ever known. His uncanny ability to sense her thoughts and her feelings had triggered the first stab of alarm, and when he had touched her she had felt threatened by something she neither knew nor understood. *What was it?*

Sarah had firmly believed that her rudeness to Anton would make him refrain from having anything further to do with her during his stay at Rosslee, but two days later, while she was having afternoon tea with Rose out on the hotel patio, a cattleya orchid was delivered to her. Sarah recognised the bold, legible handwriting on the envelope of the accompanying card, she had seen it for the first time on the prescription Anton had written out for her, and there was a nervous tremor in her hands when she lifted the flap of the envelope to extract the card.

'Sarah,' he had written simply, 'I know a small, quiet restaurant in Scottburgh that specialises in seafood. Unless I hear from you I shall take it that you agree to dine with me this evening, and I shall call for you at seven. Anton.

Sarah fingered the petals of the single, magnificent white orchid. Anton had sent her a beautiful peace-offering, and it made her feel guilty knowing that it was *she* who had been rude to *him*. And then there was his invitation to dinner.

'The frown tells me it was Anton who sent the orchid,' Rose remarked shrewdly over the rim of her teacup, and Sarah passed her the card without speaking. 'What's the problem?' Rose demanded, passing the card back to Sarah after she had read it.

'I don't know whether I ought to accept his invitation.'

'Why shouldn't you, for heaven's sake?' Rose exploded with predictable indignation. 'It won't kill you to have dinner with him, Sarah! Climb out of that shell of yours for a change, and go and enjoy yourself!'

It sounded so natural—so easy. Go and enjoy yourself. Oh, if only she *could!* If only . . .

It was no use crying for something she could never have—Sarah had, to her detriment, discovered that a long time ago—and she sighed resignedly as she rose to her feet. 'I'll have to give it some thought.'

'Oh, by the way,' Rose stopped her before she could leave, 'Walter Morgan will give you Anton's telephone number at the chalet if you want to opt out.'

There was a challenge in that statement which did not escape Sarah, and she smiled wryly at the deceptively innocent expression on the face of the woman in the red-gold floral dress.

'Thanks for the information,' she said at length, leaving Rose out on the patio to go to her room.

Sarah was restless with indecision, and she paced the carpeted floor in her bedroom like a caged animal. If she agreed to dine with Anton he might consider it an invitation to progress to something which she wanted to avoid at all costs, but if she should 'opt out', as Rose had said, it might imply that she was a coward.

'I'm not a coward! *Dammit,* I'm not a coward!' she muttered fiercely into the silence of the room, but she wrapped her arms about herself in an unconsciously protective gesture when she considered the alternative.

My pleasures are plenty, my troubles are two.
But oh, my two troubles they reave me of rest,
The brains in my head and the heart in my breast.

That fragment of a half-forgotten poem filtered into her thoughts, and it was so apt that she wanted to laugh. Her rational mind was warning her to stay away, but her heart seemed to be saying something to the contrary, and she had to face up to the fact that she was tempted.

Anton might have succeeded in angering her with his probing questions, but he had also succeeded in arousing her curiosity and her interest. She could not lie to herself. She wanted to see him again, to talk with him, and to discover, if she could, what it was about this man that had made her feel threatened.

Her mind was still shouting out warnings, but Sarah was no longer listening. She was going to accept Anton's invitation to dine with him at that small, quiet restaurant he had mentioned.

She dressed with care that evening. Not too smart and not too casual, but chic, she decided. Her choice fell on a black chiffon and satin outfit. She always looked good in black, and the pleated skirt and the top with the pencil-thin shoulder-straps looked perfect when she studied herself critically in the full-length mirror. She had acquired a smooth golden tan since her arrival at Rosslee, and that set the garment off to perfection.

What Sarah did not notice before she turned away from the mirror was that the outfit enhanced her femininity by accentuating the graceful arch from her slender neck down to her shoulders, the gentle thrust of her breasts, and the faintly seductive curve of her hips.

The overall picture was that of a self-confident, elegant, and stunningly attractive woman. There was a promise of passion in the curl of her upper lip and a distinct sensuality in the fluidity of her movements, but she would not have recognised these qualities in herself even if they had been pointed out to her.

Sarah had pampered herself with a leisurely scented bath before dressing that evening. It had left her feeling relaxed in mind as well as body, but a strange excitement was beginning to stir inside her when she seated herself at the dressing-table to add the final touches to her make-up. She felt like a teenager preparing to go out on her first date, and that was ridiculous, she reprimanded herself fiercely as she replaced the cap on her coral-pink lipstick.

She brushed her hair vigorously until it shone before she coiled it into its usual neat chignon. She reached for her combs, but for some obscure reason she changed her mind, and released the silken, gold-brown mass to fall free to her shoulders. She swept the thick strands of hair back against her temples instead, and secured them at the back of her head with a diamanté-studded clip.

Rose would approve, she thought, smiling to herself as she fastened a single string of pearls about her throat. The pearls had been a gift from her godfather on her twenty-first birthday. It had also been the only gift she had received on that day.

I'm ready, she thought, slipping her stockinged feet into gold high-heeled sandals and checking the contents of her evening purse, but she was not so sure what exactly she was ready for.

The telephone rang a few minutes later and Sarah glanced at her watch as she walked quickly towards the marble-topped bedside pedestal to lift the receiver. It was five past seven! Had Anton changed his mind?

'Miss Courtney?' the girl on the switchboard queried.

'Yes?'

'Dr de Ville is waiting for you in the foyer,' the girl said.

'I'll be down in a minute.'

Sarah was taking the bend in the stairs when she saw Anton's tall, muscular frame leaning against the reception counter, and her heart fluttered in her breast like a wild bird trapped in a small cage. His hair had been brushed back severely from his broad forehead, and his blue blazer looked as if it had been tailored to accommodate the width of his powerful shoulders. His lean hips and long limbs were encased in grey trousers, and he crossed the foyer in a few lithe strides to await her at the bottom of the stairs.

He watched her descend the last few steps, his eyes moving over her in a way that made her feel as if he was actually touching her, and a quivering warmth erupted deep inside her to spread swiftly throughout her body until it felt as if her skin was tingling. Sarah had never experienced anything quite so physical before, and her legs felt strangely weak when he took her hand and drew it through his arm.

His compelling glance captured hers, and she prayed that her eyes would not reveal the confusion reigning inside her. 'I'm a bit late,' he said.

'I noticed.'

'Clock-watcher!' he accused mockingly, and Sarah could not suppress the gurgle of nervous laughter that passed her lips.

'Old habits die hard,' she explained as they crossed

the foyer towards the exit.

'Every second counts, does it?'

'Timing is often vitally important.' She looked up then, and something in his eyes made her add hastily, 'In business.'

'I appreciate the clarification,' he laughed shortly, and seconds later the balmy night air washed up against her as they left the hotel and walked round to the side of the building where Anton had parked his car.

The sleek dark blue Jaguar was a perfect match for Anton. Dangerous and powerful were the two adjectives that came to mind to describe the vehicle and its owner, and Sarah felt ridiculously like a fly being lured into a trap when Anton held open the door on the passenger side. His hand was beneath her elbow, his splayed fingers like fire against her skin as he helped her into the car, and a pulse leapt jerkily at the base of her throat when he finally released her and closed the door.

She tried to focus her attention on the cushioned comfort of the car during the drive to Scottburgh, but having to share the closeted interior of the Jaguar with a man like Anton suggested an intimacy that made her nerves flare in alarm.

Sarah was much too aware of that strong hand with the long, flat-tipped fingers which almost brushed against her knee every time he had to change gear, and she could no longer ignore that powerful aura of masculinity which surrounded him. The woman in her recognised it and, for the first time in her life, responded to it.

She felt panicky with the discovery that she had ventured on to unfamiliar terrain, and she broke the silence between them in a desperate attempt to hide her discomfiture. She talked about the weather, and the traffic on the N2. She talked about anything and everything she could think of which might lessen that inexplicable awareness of the man seated beside her in the darkened interior of the car. Anton contributed to the conversation in an easy, relaxed manner, but Sarah had a nasty suspicion that he had not been fooled for a moment by her sudden bout of loquaciousness.

The seafood restaurant in the seaside town of Scottburgh was tucked away at the far end of an alley between two buildings, and it was small and quiet with a mere handful of diners occupying the tables.

'The peak season starts in December, and then this place is usually overcrowded,' Anton explained while they were being shown to a table in an alcove beside a window overlooking the Indian Ocean.

They sipped at the dry white wine Anton had ordered and ate their fruit cocktail while they waited for their langoustines to be served, and this time it was Anton who initiated the conversation, but finally he too lapsed into a silence which threatened to become awkward.

Sarah looked out of the window, her glance shifting absently into the distance where she could see the flickering lights of a passing ship. There were several other ships closer to shore, lying at anchor while they awaited their turn to enter the Durban harbour, but she barely noticed them. There was something that needed to be said, and there was no sense in delaying it, she decided when she met Anton's narrowed blue gaze across the small, candlelit table with the red checked cloth draped over it.

'Anton, I would——'

Sarah, I must——'

They broke off abruptly, and there was a brief embarrassed silence before their laughter eased the tension between them.

'You first,' Anton conceded with a hint of laughter still lurking in his eyes, but Sarah's expression had sobered considerably.

'I wanted to apologise for my rudeness the other morning,' she said, and the laughter left his eyes to leave his expression grave.

'I was going to apologise to *you*, Sarah,' he confessed with a rueful grimace. 'I overstepped the mark, and I deserved everything I got.'

Their eyes met and held, and something passed between them; something which left Sarah with the feeling that an invisible bond had been forged between them. It unnerved her, but it also made the blood pulse a little faster through her veins.

'I haven't thanked you for the orchid,' she said with an unfamiliar breathlessness in her husky voice.

'I haven't told you how lovely you are.' His hand covered hers where it lay on the checked tablecloth, and his light touch was infinitely disturbing. 'You are, you know,' he added when he saw the pink tide of embarrassment rising in her cheeks. 'You're a very attractive woman.'

Her smile was tainted with sarcasm, and she almost snatched her hand from beneath his to curl her trembling fingers about the stem of her wine glass. 'Your assurance is appreciated, but I've come a long way from the gauche nineteen-year-old girl who thought she was plain.'

Anton raised a mocking eyebrow, but he did not

comment on her statement, and moments later the waiter arrived with the small lobsters they had ordered.

The remainder of that evening was not the ordeal Sarah had envisaged. Anton did not question her unduly, and neither did he prompt her to talk about herself. He kept their conversation light and entertaining throughout their meal, and Sarah was in a miraculously calm, relaxed mood when he finally took her back to the hotel.

Having dinner with Anton that evening was only the beginning, and Sarah saw him almost every day during the next two weeks. She could hardly have avoided him in a place as small as Rosslee, it would have been foolish of her to try, and neither had she wanted to. He had succeeded in capturing her interest, and she had become intensely curious to know more about him.

A scenic drive in the air-conditioned comfort of Anton's Jaguar usually included a stop for lunch somewhere at one of the better known coastal resorts, or shopping for hand-crafted mementoes at the roadside stalls. In the evenings they mostly dined together, sometimes at the seafood restaurant in Scottburgh, and occasionally at Anton's chalet when he would grill meat on an open fire in the built-in barbecue off the patio.

He also took her for long hikes which she would never have attempted on her own, introduced her to the primitive but picturesque trails that followed the coastline, and when they felt too lazy to do anything strenuous they would bathe in the safety of the hotel pool, or simply soak up the sun on the beach.

Sarah found it fascinating talking with Anton. They often disagreed on various issues, but she soon discovered that he was a man of high intellect, dedicated to his profession, and with a quick, sometimes biting sense of humour. He could make her laugh just as easily as he could make her angry, but conversing with him was always a stimulating experience and never boring.

Anton's intellect was not the only thing that attracted Sarah. There was a physical awareness between them which was often so intense that she would be afraid to look at him for fear her eyes might reveal the alien emotions stirring inside her, and there were times when she had the strongest conviction that he felt the same.

'You've been spending quite a lot of time with Anton de Ville these past two weeks,' Rose remarked one scorchingly hot afternoon when Sarah joined her for tea out on the hotel patio where they could enjoy the benefit of the cool breeze blowing in from the shore.

'Yes, I have been seeing quite a lot of Anton,' Sarah admitted readily, and a triumphant little smile flashed across Rose's lined face.

'I said you'd enjoy his company, didn't I?'

'It's more than that, it's . . . oh, I don't know.' Sarah combed her fingers agitatedly through her hair which she had left free of its confining combs, and somehow her feelings spilled unrehearsed from her lips. 'Being with Anton is like finding the threads of the person I once used to be and trying to link them up to the person I am now. Does that sound crazy to you?'

'Not at all,' Rose assured her gravely. 'We sometimes tend to get lost within ourselves as a form of self-preservation.'

'But that's a cowardly thing to do.'

'It's cowardly only if we never pause to acknowledge it.'

Sarah considered this in silence while she drank her

tea. It was possible, she supposed, that she had got lost somewhere within herself as a form of self-preservation. She had endured enough pain and humiliation in the past to last her a lifetime, hadn't she?

'Will you have time for a game of chess this evening?' Rose interrupted her speculative thoughts, and Sarah shook her head ruefully.

'I'm afraid not, Rose,' she apologised. 'Anton has invited me out to dinner.'

CHAPTER FIVE

THE seafood restaurant in Scottburgh was unusually crowded that evening, but Anton had reserved their favourite table in the alcove beside the window overlooking the ocean. They ordered grilled soles and sipped at a white wine while they waited, but Sarah was incapable of shedding her uneasiness despite the relaxed, jovial atmosphere in the restaurant. She had sensed an unfamiliar tension in Anton when he had collected her at the hotel, and she detected it again now in the brooding glance that met hers across the table.

'How old were you when your mother died?' he questioned her unexpectedly, and Sarah went rigid.

'Is this going to be an inquisition?' she demanded with her customary reluctance to open the doors to her past.

'We've talked about everything except you these past two weeks because that's the way you've wanted it, but now I'd like to know more about you.' He lifted the bottle of wine from its bed of ice and topped up their glasses. 'If my questions should become too personal you may tell me to mind my own business, and I'll try not to be offended.'

He was laughing at her now, she could see it in his eyes, but he had meant it when he had said she could tell him to mind his own business, and Sarah relented on the strength of that statement.

'My mother was apparently never a very strong woman, and she died when I was eight,' she said, curling her fingers about the stem of her glass.

'Your father never married again, did he?'

'No.' She sipped at her wine and the tension eased slightly out of her body as she cast her mind back. 'My father had very little time and patience with women, and I've often wondered if his marriage to my mother was a happy one.'

Anton studied her intently, his rapier-sharp glance observing every expression that flitted across her face. 'Your father must have found it extremely difficult bringing up a child on his own.'

Sarah hastily suppressed the unexpected desire to laugh and said bluntly, 'He packed me off to a convent and left my upbringing to the nuns.'

'And that hurt.'

Anton had summed up the situation with that uncanny ability of his to see beneath the veneer of indifference she had adopted over the years, and she knew it would be fatal to deny it.

'I suppose, in a way, it did hurt, but mostly I felt bewildered and lost.'

Why am I telling him this? What's it got to do with him? she wondered agitatedly.

'I'm sure your father did what he considered was best for you at the time,' Anton remarked in a placating manner, his hand finding hers across the table.

'I don't doubt that,' she conceded.

Her eyes were on that strong, sun-browned hand covering hers. It was perhaps his intention to comfort her, but the air between them was suddenly crackling with an emotional tension that made her pulses react wildly to that thumb caressing the back of her wrist. She was about to jerk her hand free, but she looked up at that moment, and something in Anton's eyes stayed her action.

He wanted her! This was not the first time she had seen his eyes darkening with desire, but he had never made it so obvious before.

His fiery glance rested for a moment on that erratic pulse at the base of her throat before it shifted lower to the agitated rise and fall of her breasts beneath the shimmering silk of her strapless crimson dress, then he looked up, capturing her glance and holding it relentlessly. If he had wanted visible evidence of the effect he was having on her, then the mocking quirk of his mouth told her he had found it, and she could almost hate him for being so observant.

'Let go of my hand,' she pleaded huskily, but she might just as well have asked the building to collapse on her.

He uncurled her fingers effortlessly and raised her hand to his mouth to explore her soft palm with his tongue, and it was such an erotic caress that the aching heat of desire erupting in her loins made her gasp audibly.

Desire? Was that surge of feeling desire? Sarah was too confused to be sure. She was, however, sure of one thing. During the past two weeks there had been instances when she had not recognised herself as the cool, controlled woman she knew herself to be, and at that precise moment her emotions were in a frantic riot. She knew she had to do something about it, but nothing in her past had equipped her to deal with something such as this.

Out of the corner of her eye she could see the waiter making his way towards their table with the soles they had ordered, and she heaved an inward sigh of relief when Anton was forced to release her hand. He leaned back in his chair while their meal was placed before them, but there was a gleam of triumph in his eyes when his glance shifted from her flushed cheeks down to that erratic pulse which was still throbbing at the base of her throat.

The moment had passed, allowing Sarah sufficient time to regain her much-needed composure while they concentrated on their food, and it was Anton who did most of the talking while they ate. He regaled her with amusing anecdotes drawn from personal experiences in the medical profession which evoked her laughter, and afterwards, as they lingered at the table over a cup of coffee, she was too pleasantly relaxed to object when Anton reverted to the conversation they had had earlier.

'Did you have a good relationship with your father?' he asked, and Sarah's expression sobered instantly.

'Not really,' she said, staring down into the cup of aromatic coffee in front of her while she searched for the right words with which to describe Edmond Courtney. 'My father was an autocratic and often overbearing man,' she explained at length. 'He always made it very difficult for me to get to know him, and he was exceptionally hard to please.'

'He made you feel inadequate.'

Sarah's head shot up, her startled glance meeting Anton's across the flickering flame of the candle which was burning low between them. 'I never said that!'

His calm statement had cut through her defences. Anton was not a fool, he had seen too much already, and there was no sense in attempting to evade the truth.

'Yes, my father made me feel inadequate,' she

confessed, her tawny eyes defying him to mock her, but there was no sign of mockery in the glance that held hers, only compassionate understanding.

'I think . . .' his eyes were narrowed and intent upon her face as he leaned towards her across the circular table, '. . . I'm the first person to whom you've ever admitted that.'

'You are,' she admitted, forcing the words past her tight aching throat.

It was odd, but having made that confession to Anton seemed to lift a great weight off her shoulders. It also left her feeling exposed and vulnerable, and she hastily lowered her eyes only to find herself staring at his strong, deeply tanned throat.

His white, open-necked shirt had been left unbuttoned far enough for her to glimpse the dark chest hair curling against his skin. It looked soft and springy, and she wondered idly what it would feel like to run her fingers through it, to touch his warm skin and to . . .

God, what am I thinking?

Sarah looked away, her heart thudding heavily against her breastbone while she forcibly channelled her thoughts in a different direction, but she could not suppress the wave of heat that surged into her cheeks, and she could only pray that Anton would attribute her embarrassment to the confession she had made.

'My father also had the ability to exercise a certain charm which successfully won people over to his way of thinking.' Sarah might have been outwardly in control of herself once again, but on the inside she was a quivering mass of conflicting emotions. 'That was perhaps the most vital key to his success,' she elaborated, 'but I think I always admired my father most for his brilliant and innovative mind.'

'Two qualities which you've obviously inherited,' Anton observed quietly, his compelling glance drawing Sarah's.

'I shall take that as a compliment.'

His gaze sharpened on the innocently provocative smile curving her attractive mouth, but his expression became hooded when he sensed her withdrawal. 'Did you father encourage you to take an interest in the business?'

'Oh, no! Never!' She shook her head and, for the first time, laughed at the memory. 'I was a raw ignoramus when my dear godfather persuaded me into the business after my father's death.'

'It must have been tough.'

'It was,' she admitted, resting her elbows on the table and staring out of the window beside her.

Ships lay at anchor in the sea, their lights reflected on the water, but further out there was nothing to be seen except the moon bathing the ocean with its silvery glow. It was a tranquil scene, but it was in direct contrast with the memories that were beginning to flood Sarah's mind at that moment.

'I worked almost day and night for eight gruelling months,' she explained, dragging her glance away from the moonlit landscape beyond the window to find Anton observing her silently and intently. 'I started at the bottom and I plodded my way up, but it was worth it in the end.'

'I would say you've proved yourself extremely capable as your father's successor, and I'm sure he would have been proud of you.'

'Perhaps,' she agreed absently.

Her best had never been good enough for Edmond Courtney. Would her father have been proud of her now? Or would he have weighed her achievements and found them wanting? She would never know.

Anton was staring at the lustrous string of pearls which she wore about her throat, and Sarah's hand instinctively followed the direction of his gaze as if, subconsciously, she needed to reassure herself that it was still there.

Blue eyes narrowed perceptibly. 'You've worn those pearls several times. Is it a gift from an admirer?'

'Yes.' Her smile mocked Anton's curiosity. 'My godfather.'

That unfathomable hint of jealous anger in his eyes faded rapidly. 'You're very fond of him.'

'I love him dearly,' she admitted, her expression softening.

'I know he feels the same way about you.'

Sarah did not need to be told how her godfather felt about her; she had never once doubted that she possessed his unconditional love and support. He had long ago become the much-needed anchor in her life, and for this he would always have her love, her respect, and her undying gratitude.

'More coffee?'

She emerged swiftly from her thoughts and shook her head. 'I've had more than enough, thank you.'

'It's time I took you back to the hotel.' Anton pushed back his chair and rose to his feet, his rugged features grave as he held out his hand to her. 'I've kept you out much later than I intended, and you still need to get as much rest as possible.'

Sarah did not quibble. She had revealed more to

Anton in this one evening than to anyone else in her entire life, and it was this disquieting discovery that kept her silent in the car during the drive back to Rosslee.

It was eleven-thirty when they arrived at the hotel. Sarah collected her key at the reception desk and turned to Anton. She did not want him to escort her up to her room, she wanted to end the evening there in the foyer, but it seemed as if he was locked into her thoughts.

'I'll see you safely to your room,' he forestalled her with a hint of mockery in his eyes, and her protest was stifled in her throat when his warm, strong hand settled supportively beneath her elbow. 'Do you play tennis?' he wanted to know as he ushered her up the stairs.

'I play occasionally when I have the time,' she answered him in a deceptively calm voice. 'Why do you ask?'

'The hotel has a perfectly good tennis-court just begging to be used, and if you don't have anything else planned for tomorrow afternoon then I thought you might like to join me for a couple of friendly games.'

Tennis! Sarah's nervousness abated slightly. She would enjoy a few games of tennis. It was years since she had last indulged in sport of any kind, but she had arrived at Rosslee with an ill-equipped wardrobe for the sporting facilities the hotel had to offer.

'I didn't think to bring any tennis gear with me,' she told Anton with a rueful grimace when they reached the upper floor and turned right along the dimly lit passage that led to her room.

'You'll get tennis shoes at the shop just up the road from the hotel, and I happen to have a spare racket at the chalet which you're welcome to use.'

'I shall look forward to tomorrow, then.' She smiled

up at him as they stopped outside her bedroom. 'What time?'

'Three-thirty,' he said, taking her key from her to unlock the door. 'I'll meet you at the tennis-court,' he added as the white panelled door swung open beneath his hand.

Sarah nodded in agreement, her throat too constricted to speak. Anton was standing too close to her for comfort. His spicy aftershave was pleasantly assaulting her senses, and something in the expression that flitted across his ruggedly handsome face made her pulse-rate quicken in anticipation, but she hastily stifled the feeling.

'Goodnight, Anton,' she said politely. 'And thank you for a lovely evening.'

She turned away from him, wanting to escape into the safety of her room before she made a fool of herself, but his arm shot out to bar her way, and she sagged back against the door-jamb, her eyes dilating as she saw his glance resting purposefully on her lips.

'Don't be afraid, Sarah,' he said softly, his hands sliding about her waist as he backed her into the moonlit darkness of her room and closed the door behind him with his foot.

Afraid? That was not how Sarah would have described her feelings at that moment when Anton took her evening purse from her hand and flung it on to a nearby chair. He was going to kiss her. This was something she had feared for almost two weeks, but she also wanted it so much at that moment that she was almost too afraid to breathe when he raised a hand to trail his fingers across her cheek. He tilted her face up to his, and her heart was suddenly beating so hard and fast in her throat that it almost succeeded in cutting off her air supply.

'Don't be afraid,' he murmured again, his hand at her waist sliding down over her buttocks to draw her body up against his own, and his face was no more than a dark shadow when he lowered his head to hers.

For a fraction of a second everything seemed to still inside Sarah as she waited and wondered. She knew from past experience what to expect, but she could not help wishing that just this once . . .

Anton's warm mouth shifted sensuously over hers, testing, tasting and tantalising her lips until they quivered in response, and then an aching warmth erupted deep down inside her. It flung her mind into total confusion. She had always believed that, sexually, she was a cold lump of flesh, but Anton was somehow arousing feelings and sensations she had thought herself incapable of, and they were so ecstatically sweet that she wanted this moment never to end.

Her control slipped. She opened her mouth to Anton's, her hands sliding up across his broad chest until her fingers locked in the short dark hair at the nape of his neck as she welcomed the erotic invasion of his tongue, and she was beginning to feel faint with an unfamiliar longing when his mouth left hers to trail a path of sensuous fire down along her throat and across her bare shoulder.

His hands explored her body through the thin silk of her dress, his fingers lingering at her breasts to caress their hard peaks, and a sweet, fiery heat surged into her loins.

'I want you, Sarah,' he groaned as he sought her mouth again with his, but those four words were sufficient to drag her back to sanity with a staggering swiftness.

What's happening to me? she asked herself a little wildly. What the hell am I doing?

Anton sensed her sudden withdrawal, and Sarah backed away from him like a startled rabbit the moment he set her free. Her face was pale in the moonlight that filtered into her bedroom through the open window, and he could not have failed to see the confusion and fear in her dilated eyes.

'What's wrong, Sarah?' he demanded with a calmness she envied at that moment.

'Nothing! It's nothing!' The words came hissingly through her clenched teeth. 'Please go! *Please!*'

She thought for one fearful moment that he was going to ignore her plea, but he turned and opened the door so that the dim passage light fell across the carpeted floor into her bedroom.

'I'll see you tomorrow,' he said, his face an unfathomable mask, and then he left, closing the door quietly behind him.

Sarah fumbled the safety latch into position, the sharp click jarring her raw nerves, and she sagged heavily against the door to take stock of herself. She was trembling all over as if she had a fever, and her heart was thudding so heavily against her ribs that it was actually painful.

Those moments in Anton's arms had been an exciting revelation. Sarah was not quite sure how to interpret her reaction, and she was still much too sceptical to believe she had lost the frigidity which had aroused Nigel's stinging contempt. She dared not explore the possibilities in this instance. Anton was not a man who would take kindly to being played with, and to become emotionally involved with someone like him could only lead to more pain.

Her lips were still tingling in the aftermath of his kisses, and the touch of his hands lingered on her body like an ecstatic and incredible memory. It had been a beautiful awakening of emotions she had not known she possessed, but she still had no knowledge of their true strength, and she wished . . .

No! It must never happen again! Sarah flicked the switch against the wall to flood the room with light while she battled to suppress the emotions which were still clamouring through her body. She would have to be more cautious in future. She must never allow him to get that close again! If he knew . . . If he should find out . . . Dear God, he would despise her for what she was!

Sarah crawled into bed half an hour later. She had taken one of the tablets Anton had prescribed for her, her eyelids already felt heavy, and she was asleep seconds after she had switched off the bedside light.

Rose Poole gave her coffee a vigorous stir while she observed Sarah intently across the breakfast table. 'You came in late last night.'

Sarah looked up from her cheese omelette and smiled wryly. 'Don't tell me you waited up to be sure I arrived home safely, Rose?'

'It was so hot last night that I couldn't sleep, and I was catching a breath of fresh air at the window when you arrived.' Rose gestured impatiently as if she could no longer contain her curiosity. 'You look a bit peaky this morning. Didn't the evening live up to your expectations?'

'It was a pleasant and enlightening evening,' Sarah answered her cautiously but truthfully. 'We're playing tennis this afternoon.'

'Ah!' A smile of satisfaction brightened Rose's expression. 'I can see Anton has cracked your shell these past two weeks, so crawl out all the way, Sarah, and have fun, my child.'

Sarah promptly lost her appetite, and when Rose left the dining-room a few minutes later, she pushed her half-eaten omelette aside and helped herself to a cup of coffee.

Cracked her shell?

The memory of last night was still alarmingly vivid, and she passed an agitated hand over her hair which she had tied back that morning with a brightly coloured scarf in the nape of her neck. Yes, Anton had certainly succeeded in cracking her shell, and in the process he had given her a taste of something which she was still too afraid to accept, but she was still far too hesitant to crawl out all the way and have fun, as Rose had suggested. Someone could get hurt, and she did not apply that solely to herself. If Anton was hurt, *she* would be hurt, and that was something she wanted to avoid at all costs.

She took a stroll up to the shop after breakfast to purchase a pair of tennis shoes, and while she was there she bought a few other necessary items, including a wide-brimmed, locally made grass hat to shade her face and neck from the damaging rays of the sun.

She paused for a moment to study herself in the full-length mirror which was tucked away in the corner among all the bric-à-brac in the crowded shop, and there was laughter in the tawny eyes peering out at her from beneath the wide brim of the grass hat. In a sleeveless khaki shirt, knee-length khaki shorts and with leather thongs on her feet she was almost unrecognisable as the elegant and sophisticated Sarah Courtney whom the media had become acquainted with over the past few years.

If they could see me now! she thought humorously when she finally left the air-conditioned shop with her purchases.

The humidity enfolded her like a damp, heated blanket the minute she stepped outside, and she was in a hurry to get back to the hotel when she heard someone call her name. Angela Morgan was walking briskly towards her from the direction of the post office, and Sarah waited with a touch of impatience for the slender, well-dressed woman to catch up to her.

'I hope you've been enjoying your stay here at Rosslee?' Angela enquired a little breathlessly as she fell into step beside Sarah.

'I've enjoyed the past four weeks very much, thank you. It's peaceful and quiet here at Rosslee, and that's what I needed most.'

'We refer to this time of the year as "the calm before the storm",' laughed Angela. 'Things usually liven up to a hectic pace at the hotel from about the middle of December all the way through to the end of January.'

'I shall be gone before then,' said Sarah.

'So you will.' Angela cast a brief but speculative glance at Sarah as they followed the road down to the hotel. 'I've noticed that Anton de Ville has been squiring you around since his arrival at Rosslee.'

'Yes, he has,' replied Sarah, instantly on the alert.

'He's a truly wonderful man, and never reluctant to offer his services when someone is ill, but I wouldn't trust him anywhere near my daughter,' Angela announced unexpectedly as they approached the entrance of the hotel. 'He's much too sexy.'

Sarah was startled. '*Sexy*' was a word frequently used in the fashion trade. She had heard it bandied about to describe various garments, but she had always shut herself off from its deeper meaning, and she did so now by hastily dismissing the issue from her mind.

'Do you have a daughter, Mrs Morgan?' she asked.

'No, I don't,' Angela confessed readily. 'I have two sons, but if Anton de Ville can make my heart flutter in his presence, then I'd hate to think what he would have done to my daughter if I'd had one!'

Angela Morgan's brand of logic was amusing, but it was also vaguely disturbing. Was she, in her own peculiar way, trying to warn Sarah about something?

Sarah wondered about this later that morning as she emerged from the pool after a refreshing swim. 'I wouldn't trust him anywhere near my daughter,' Angela had said, and, if Sarah had to be honest, she did not trust *herself* with Anton. It was a startling discovery, but it was true, and she doubted that she would trust herself again after the way she had behaved the previous evening.

She had changed into white shorts and a sleeveless apricot-coloured blouse when she went down to meet Anton that afternoon, and her heart lifted oddly in her breast when she saw him waiting for her at a table beneath one of the shady flame trees which surrounded the tennis-court. He rose to his feet when he saw her, his powerful frame clad in a white T-shirt, shorts and tennis shoes, and Sarah was suddenly incredibly nervous.

'Am I late?' she asked, her husky voice deceptively calm when she joined him.

'I'm early.' His blue eyes were watchful, but his stern mouth twitched with a suggestion of a smile. 'Timing is important, remember?' he reminded her of the remark she had passed that very first evening he had taken her out to dinner.

'So it is,' she agreed stiffly as she seated herself in the cane chair he had pulled out for her.

'You missed the sunrise this morning.'

Have you resorted to spying on me? That indignant query rose sharply to her lips as she watched him draw a chair closer to hers and sit down, but she bit it back and said instead, 'I woke up late.'

'When I didn't see you on the beach I was afraid you wouldn't keep our date this afternoon.'

Anton was being subtle, but the innuendo behind that statement was very clear. He was steering towards a topic for discussion which she had known would be unavoidable. She could not behave the way she had done the previous evening and then not expect him to demand an explanation.

Her gaze dropped to his muscled thighs and strong calves and lingered for a moment on the fine dark hair springing from his tanned skin. He was close enough for her to touch him if she altered her position slightly, and the desire to reach out to him was suddenly so intense that she had to clasp her hands tightly in her lap. She looked away hastily to focus her attention on something else, and in this instance it was the mynah birds strutting across the neatly cropped grass in search of insects.

'Anton . . . about last night——' she began uncomfortably.

'Yes, Sarah, *about* last night,' he cut in smoothly when she faltered. 'You're an attractive, desirable woman, and I'm not going to deny that I wanted you.'

'Don't say that!'

'I was not unaware of your existence before we met, I'd seen photos of you often enough, but seeing you in the flesh is something different, and I think I've wanted you almost from the first moment you walked into my consulting-room. ' Anton's ruthless honesty shocked Sarah into a stunned silence. 'I know that sounds unethical, but it's true,' he continued unperturbed, 'and I couldn't believe my luck when I discovered you were staying here at Rosslee. I didn't intend to rush you last night, and I admit that the situation got a little out of hand, but one moment you were responding beautifully and the next you froze.' The ensuing silence was almost deafening before he asked tersely, 'What happened, Sarah? What went wrong?'

I was afraid of this strange physical awareness between us. I was afraid of the feelings you were arousing, and I was afraid they would expose me for the cold, sexually worthless woman I am.

Sarah could have said all those things, and much more, but instead she heard herself stammering foolishly, 'I didn't——I don't want to——to get involved.'

'With me in particular?'

She shook her head, the dappled sunlight striking gold fire into her hair which she had tied away from her face with a white scarf. 'Not with *any* man,' she stressed huskily.

'Why not?'

'I have my reasons,' she answered him coldly, her features under control at last when she looked at him, and their glances clashed like two swords locked in deadly battle.

'Well, I've got news for you, Sarah!' The harshness in his voice made her flinch inwardly when he rose abruptly to lean over her with his hands gripping the arms of her chair, and she swallowed convulsively when she saw the ominous, angry fire in the eyes blazing down into hers. 'I'm not going to be brushed off that easily, and I have my reasons for that too!'

CHAPTER SIX

ANTON'S statement echoed threateningly through Sarah's mind. 'I'm not going to be brushed off that easily, and I have my reasons for that too!'

He meant it, she could see it in the resolute set of his strong, square jaw, and a wave of helplessness engulfed her. 'Oh, please, Anton, I wish you wouldn't——'

'We'll resume this discussion some other time,' he cut in sharply, straightening to collect the rackets and tennis balls he had left on a vacant chair. 'Shall we start?' he asked, selecting a racket and thrusting it into her hands.

Sarah sighed inwardly and nodded. 'We might as well.'

She tested the grip of the racket while they walked on to the court, and realised instantly that it could never have been used by a man. The racket she was holding had belonged to a woman. Had it been left behind and forgotten after a few passionate weeks at the chalet with Anton? It was none of her business, but she could not help wondering.

'Are you ready?' Anton called out impatiently when they had been slamming the balls across the net several times to acquire the feel of the court.

'Yes, I'm ready,' she replied, thrusting aside her thoughts and her fears to concentrate on the game.

Anton took the first service, his leniency obvious until he had tested Sarah's strength, but after that first game he showed her no mercy. His powerful services and driving shots would have crushed a lesser player, but Sarah rose to the challenge with all the agility and expertise that she could muster. She matched Anton's strength with cunning, gaining points with well-placed shots, and after an hour of strenuous play they left the court with an equal number of games to their credit.

Sarah had not exerted herself so much in years. The blood was pumping through her veins at a bracing, invigorating pace, and she felt alive again as they collapsed into their chairs and laughed at each other with that easy camaraderie which had existed between them before the emotional fiasco of the previous evening. It was something she had never experienced with any man except Anton, and it was an oddly pleasant feeling. It was a sharing, she thought, but she did not dwell on it.

Playing tennis for an hour in that hot humid climate had left them perspiring freely as if they had been caught in an unexpected downpour, and they were dabbing at their faces and necks with their hand towels when a young Indian bar steward placed a jug of iced fruit juice and glasses on their table under the flame tree. He poured juice into the two tall glasses, accepted Anton's handsome tip with a flashing smile, and left.

'I ordered this earlier while I was waiting for you,' Anton answered Sarah's unspoken query.

'That was thoughtful of you.'

They lapsed into a comfortable silence, drinking thirstily from their glasses, but Sarah was remembering his anger and the warning that he was not going to be brushed off easily. She had not imagined that it would be easy, but she had not allowed for the fact that he would make it quite so difficult for her.

'You play a much stronger game than you led me to believe,' Anton remarked with a hint of rebuke in his voice, and Sarah had been so lost in thought that it took a moment for her to realise what he was talking about.

'Tennis was my favourite sport at school,' she explained, dabbing at her hot face again with the point of the towel she had draped about her neck. 'We had a tennis-court in the grounds of our home in Cape Town, and my father often invited guests over for an afternoon of tennis, but I honestly haven't played much these past six years.' She looked up then, saw the laughter in Anton's blue eyes, and realised that he had been teasing her. 'You play a pretty forceful game yourself,' she added with mock severity. 'And that's something *you* didn't tell *me*.'

'I played tennis and cricket, and I participated in athletics during my years at school, but I started playing squash when I was at university, and that's the game I enjoy most.'

Sarah drained her glass and placed it on the table while her glance trailed briefly over his long, muscle-toned body stretched out in the chair close to hers. 'Is that how you manage to keep yourself in such superb physical condition?'

She wished she had not asked that question. It seemed so personal, almost intimate, and she felt her cheeks become heated with embarrassment when Anton grinned at her as if he had sensed her discomfiture.

'I don't always have the time for a game of squash, but I've a fully equipped gym at home where I work out regularly to rid myself of the stress and strain which accompanies my job, and other than that I spend what free time I have in my garden.'

Her eyes widened in surprise. 'You enjoy gardening?'

'I find it a relaxing hobby.'

'Amazing,' she mocked him.

'What's so amazing about it?'

The tension and the anger between them had gone, but the reason for it was still there like a tangible substance in the air. They had chosen to ignore it when they came off the court, but Sarah felt it again now as she met his compelling glance. 'I somehow never imagined you as a man who would enjoy pottering about in a garden, that's all,' she answered lamely.

'Appearances can be deceptive,' Anton mocked her in turn. 'What do you do for relaxation in your free time?'

Sarah stiffened. It was wrong of her to resent that query, but she could not help it. 'I don't have time to relax with a hobby,' she answered him truthfully.

'All work and no play.' He raised himself from his lounging position and shook his head at her. 'Sarah, what *have* you been doing to yourself?'

'I've worked hard and I've enjoyed every minute of it,' she defended herself.

'You've worked hard, I'll grant you that, but in the process you've buried yourself alive before you've even had the chance to live.'

'Don't be absurd!' she protested after a startled silence. 'I live a very full and interesting life, and if my profession has spilled over to a large extent into my personal life, then it's because I find my work stimulating and satisfying!'

'You're using Courtney's as a shield, and for some obscure reason you deliberately mapped out a tight schedule for yourself which has forced you to channel all your energy into your work these past six years. *Why,* Sarah?'

To protect myself against men like you who want to expose me to the painful side of living! she wanted to shout at him, but she controlled herself and said coldly, 'I thought you were a physician, not a psychologist.'

'Psychology has common sense as a basis, and my common sense tells me that there has to be a reason why you've been shutting yourself away from a normal physical and emotional relationship with a man,' he parried her sarcastic remark with an infuriating calmness. 'I doubt that your father has anything to do with it and I refuse to believe that you're mourning for the husband whom you said you never loved. No, it has to be something else, and I'm going to dig until I know what it is.'

'I suggest you mind your own business!' Her icy, controlled anger was the only defence she had against the fear stirring inside her.

'Don't put on that frosty act with me, Sarah,' he countered derisively. 'I'm willing to bet that underneath the icicles there's a fiercely passionate woman longing to come out, and I'm going to make it my business to find her.'

A suffocating sensation caught at her chest. 'You don't know what you're talking about.'

'Oh, yes, I do,' he smiled, his mouth curving sensuously as if the prospect of proving her wrong would delight him, and a pulse leapt nervously in her throat.

Anton saw the nervous antics of that tell-tale pulse, and his smile deepened with mockery. 'Go and put on your bathing suit and bring whatever else you may need,' he commanded as he got up to collect their things, and the clatter of tennis rackets jangled her sensitive nerves. 'We'll cool off in the tidal pool on the beach, and afterwards you can shower and change at my place.'

Sarah shook her head apprehensively. 'No, I don't think I should——'

The rest of her sentence was caught up in a gasp of surprise as he gripped her arm with his free hand and jerked her up out of her chair with a force that almost made her body collide with his.

'Do I have to march you up to your room to make sure that you do as you're told?' he demanded in an ominously quiet voice, and his face was so close to hers that she could see the faint shadow of beard along his square, determined jaw. 'Do I, Sarah?'

'No!' She shook her head and rubbed her arm gingerly when he released her. She would have bruises there tomorrow, she thought as she looked up at him accusingly. 'You're a bully!'

'I know.' He smiled briefly and placed his hand in the hollow of her back to give her a gentle push in the direction of the hotel building. 'I'll wait for you at the front entrance, and be quick about it.'

Sarah was glad to get away from Anton for a few minutes and she was almost running when she entered the hotel and went up the stairs to her room. She locked the door behind her and wished she could stay there, but she had a horrible feeling that a locked door would not prevent Anton from barging into her room if he should suspect she was not going to carry out his instructions.

She hunted for her one-piece bathing suit, but failed to find it, and then she remembered. One of the

shoulder-straps had snapped the last time she had worn
it, and the laundry-maid had taken it away that morning
to mend it.

Oh, lord, *help!* I can't wear that bikini! Not today!
Especially not today! she was thinking frantically as she
snatched up the telephone and asked the switchboard to
put her through to the laundry-room. Her bathing suit
would not be ready until much later that afternoon, she
was told, and she replaced the receiver with a sigh of
resignation to haul her bikini out of the cupboard.

She left the room ten minutes later with a small
travelling bag clutched in her hand and her swimming
towel draped casually over one shoulder. She had
exchanged tennis shoes for sandals, and it was the
clicking of their low heels on the slate patio that make
Anton turn and glance up at her with a hint of mockery
in his eyes when she began to descend the shallow steps
into the gravelled driveway.

'What took you so long?' he demanded, and she had
to suppress a nervous giggle.

'You should learn to be patient.'

'Patience has never been one of my virtues,' he said
with something close to a scowl on his face as he
relieved her of her bag. 'Come on,' he added abruptly,
taking her firmly by the hand as if he was afraid she
might change her mind and dash back into the hotel.

The tide had come in, the waves were lashing the
rocks and spilling over them to fill the natural pool.
Anton dropped their belongings on to the hot sand, took
off his tennis shoes, and pulled his T-shirt off over his
head. His tan had deepened since his arrival at Rosslee,
Sarah was thinking, her glance resting with something
close to fascination on his muscular body as he undid

the belt hugging his shorts to his lean hips and pulled down the zip. She held her breath for a heart-stopping second, her fingers stilling nervously on the buttons of her blouse, and almost sighed audibly with relief when she realised that he was suitably dressed underneath his shorts.

His black bathing briefs sat low on his hips to accentuate, as always, the perfect symmetry of his muscle-toned body, and a strange weakness assailed Sarah's limbs. She was not unused to seeing male bodies in various stages of undress, but she had never before seen one quite as magnificent as Anton's, and there was an odd tightening in her chest when she took off her blouse and raised her hands to free her thick, wavy hair from the confining scarf.

Anton stood waiting, that familiar brooding expression on his ruggedly handsome face as he watched her kick off her sandals and step out of her shorts, and Sarah wished she had had the foresight to have her one-piece suite mended a day sooner.

She felt uncomfortably naked in her scanty bikini with those narrowed brooding eyes roaming her body so freely, but if Anton could stare, then so could she, and her gaze lingered boldly on his powerful chest with the matting of dark hair that tapered down to a narrow V above his navel.

'You have a beautiful body, Sarah.'

His voice was low and throaty, his manner blatantly sexual, and the breath stilled in her throat as she felt her nipples harden beneath the stretchy blue fabric of her bikini top. She had for so many years considered her body incapable of responding to a man in a physical way without actually being touched, and it was a delightful shock to discover her error, but Anton's sensuous smile made her cheeks flame with shame as she realised that he had witnessed her arousal.

'Race you into the water!' she challenged, catching him off his guard and leaving him standing while she sprinted across the sand sloping down towards the pool.

'You're a witch!' shouted Anton, his long legs bringing him up beside her as she ran into the shallow waves to where the sand fell sharply beneath their feet, and they plunged simultaneously into the cool water which was no more than waist-deep at high tide.

They swam towards a wooden raft anchored in the centre of the pool, Anton's powerful strokes taking him ahead of Sarah, and she laughingly proclaimed him the victor when he lifted himself on to the bobbing wooden raft.

'If the race had started fairly I might have allowed you to win,' he chided her while he wiped the water out of his eyes.

'No, you wouldn't have,' she contradicted him laughingly. 'You're a winner by nature, not a loser.'

'Perhaps you should remember that,' he warned, giving an entirely different meaning to their bantering conversation.

'I shall ignore that remark,' she said, determined to enjoy the refreshing coolness and buoyancy of the seawater even though it disturbed her to know that Anton was observing her intently while she floated on her back and drifted gently with the swell.

Sarah was thinking that he looked almost boyish with his wet hair clinging to his proudly sculpted head, but there was nothing boyish about the expression that entered his eyes a few seconds later as he slid from the raft into the water and waded purposefully towards her.

'I don't take kindly to being ignored,' he announced with a devilish gleam in his eyes, and he was so dangerously, aggressively male at that moment that Sarah panicked.

It was an absurd thing to do, she realised afterwards, but at that precise moment she was conscious only of a frantic need to get away from him as quickly as possible. She lashed out towards the beach, but her actions were retarded by the water like someone caught up in a nightmare, and Anton finally brought her down with a flying tackle that drove them both under the salty water.

'Stay away from me!' she cried when she emerged, spluttering, moments later.

'I'm damned if I'll allow you to ignore me,' she heard him laughing, and she was still flicking the long strands of wet hair out of her face when she felt his arms snaking about her waist.

Her hands rose instinctively in an attempt to push him away, but instead she was clutching at his shoulders for support when the pull of the water unbalanced her, and her cry of protest was no more than a strangled moan deep down in her throat when he pulled her up against him.

Her hips and her thighs were moulded intimately to his, making it impossible for her to ignore his manhood. With Nigel every feminine instinct would have frozen into rejection at this point, but with Anton it was something quite different. A melting warmth flooded her being, sweeping aside the tension gripping her muscles, and Anton drew a shuddering breath, the laughter leaving his face as he felt her yielding response.

'God help me, but I need this, Sarah,' he groaned, his

fingers ploughing into the tangled hair at the nape of her neck, and in that instant Sarah recognised the staggering fact that she needed it too.

She tasted the salt of the sea on his lips as his mouth claimed hers, and her arms went up of their own volition until they were locked about his neck. Her breasts were hurting against his chest, but the pain did not seem to matter when he kissed her with a searing, hungry passion that stirred her to the depths of her soul. He kissed her eyelids, the tip of her nose, her cheeks, and her throat, but he returned again and again to her soft mouth as if he thirsted for something which only her lips could give him.

The roar of the sea was in Sarah's ears. Or was it the rush of her own blood through her veins? She could not decide which it was as she felt herself drifting weightless on the stormy tide of her emotions. This was new, it was exciting, and it filled her again with a burning curiosity. If Anton could arouse her body to this extent, then surely she was capable of more?

Dear God, what am I thinking? What am I doing?

'No!' she gasped, struggling frantically to free herself as she felt the slight stubble of Anton's beard scraping against the sensitive cord of her throat. Her hands were flat against the hard wall of his chest, her arm muscles aching in her attempt to push him away, but his sensuous mouth was trailing yet another devastating path along her jaw in search of her lips which were swollen and tender in the aftermath of his passionate kisses. 'That's enough!' she begged hoarsely. 'Please, Anton, that's enough!'

His arms slackened their hold for an instant, giving her the opportunity she had needed, and she pushed him away from her with an unexpected burst of strength that sent him toppling over backwards into the water. If the circumstances had not been so grave she might have found the stunned look on his face amusing, but at that moment she was in a blind panic to get away from him.

'Sarah!' There was an authoritative command in his voice, but she refused to heed it as she thrashed through the shallow water towards the beach. '*Dammit*, Sarah!' he shouted after her. 'You're the most infuriating woman I've ever met!'

She dried herself as quickly as she could and she was pulling on her shorts when Anton came out of the water and ran up the beach towards her. He was angry, she could see it in the rigid set of his jaw, but she had her emotions firmly under control again and she was calmly shaking the sand out of her blouse when she felt him coming up behind her.

'Sarah!' He spun her round to face him, his hands bitingly hard on her shoulders. 'I'm not sure I know what's going on between us, but I don't consider it a game!'

'Neither do I,' she said gravely, raising her glance from the strong column of his throat to see him blink as if she had given him a sobering slap in the face.

'Well, at least we're in agreement on that!'

He released her abruptly and turned away to put on his white shorts, and Sarah stared dumbly at his broad, muscled back, her gaze riveted to the drops of moisture glistening on his tanned skin while she shrugged herself into her blouse and fastened the buttons.

Oh, if only life could have been less complicated! she was thinking as they collected their belongings in silence and walked up the beach to the chalet. If only she could have the courage to explore the extent of those feelings Anton aroused in her. If only she *dared*!

'You're of no use to any man!'

Sarah shivered at the memory of those words which Nigel had flung at her shortly after she had been dismissed from the hospital. For almost eight years she had borne that accusation like a cross, believing in it, but now she was not so sure. She had been anything but cold and unresponsive when Anton had kissed her, but she was still too wary to trust the emotions he had aroused in her.

The air-conditioned interior of Anton's chalet was a welcome reprieve from the heat and the humidity which prevailed outside, but Sarah felt awkward and tense, and she could not enjoy the coolness of the air filtering through the rooms when Anton ushered her upstairs.

'Use this bathroom,' he said curtly, not looking at her as he paused on the upper landing to push open one of the doors. 'I'll use the bathroom off the main bedroom.'

Sarah tried to think of something to say which would ease the strain and the tension between them, but he was striding away from her before she could find the right words, and there was a sinking feeling in her chest when she finally entered the blue and white tiled bathroom and closed the door behind her.

She showered quickly and washed the sand out of her hair with the small bottle of shampoo she had brought with her, and she left a small towel wrapped around her head when she finally dressed herself in the beige cotton skirt and white blouse she had brought with her. She rubbed her hair vigorously with the towel, drying it as much as she could before she combed it into some sort of order, and the only make-up she used on her face was a dab of powder, an eyeliner, and a light touch of the coral-pink lipstick she favoured.

Sarah had been blessed with a healthy, flawless skin which needed very little make-up to accentuate her high cheekbones, the wide-set eyes and generous, sensuously curved mouth, but she was not thinking about her appearance when she stared at her reflected image in the small mirror above the hand basin. She was thinking about Anton, and acknowledging the fact that he had been understandably angry. Her capricious behaviour these past two days was enough to confuse and anger anyone. How could she explain her actions to Anton when she could not even explain them to herself?

Her life had been orderly and controlled these past six years. Why did Anton de Ville have to come along and fling it into chaos? Sarah sighed exasperatedly as she picked up her bag and checked that the bathroom was tidy before she went downstairs.

She heard someone moving about in the kitchen, and she was straightening from placing her bag on the carpeted floor beside a chair when Anton walked into the lounge in faded blue denims and a white, short-sleeved shirt which was unbuttoned almost to his waist.

His glance flicked over her and sharpened briefly on the slight tremor in the hands she clasped nervously in front of her, but his expression remained inscrutable as he gestured with the tray he was carrying. 'I've made coffee.'

'Thanks, that will be nice,' she said, trying to sound calm and natural despite the nervous flutter at the pit of her stomach as she watched him put the tray down on the low circular table between the chairs.

He slid a tape into the deck of the portable radio/tape player which stood on the small pine table against the wall. He switched it on, and they helped themselves to a cup of coffee while the soft strains of a violin concerto filled the room.

Sarah concentrated on the music and tried desperately to relax while they drank their coffee, but the emotional tension between them was like a string which had been pulled too taut, and it seemed to be dangerously close to snapping.

'It was most discourteous of me not to ask,' Anton finally broke the strained silence between them. 'Do you like classical music?'

'Mozart is one of my favourite composers,' she confessed, catching a look of surprise on his face. 'I have quite a collection of classical records at my flat.'

His eyes mocked her as he drained his cup and leaned forward to put it on the tray. 'Are they gathering dust on the shelves? Or do you actually have the time to listen to them?'

Three weeks ago Sarah might have lost her temper at this deliberate dig, but now she simply chose to ignore it. 'I often take work home in the evenings, and working to music seems to ease the strain of what I'm doing, but I seldom have time these days to sit down and simply listen to them.'

'My taste in music is varied, and over the years I've managed to amass an interesting collection of records and tapes.' Anton looked relaxed where he sat stretched out in his chair with his fingers laced together across his wide chest, but Sarah sensed that every muscle in that magnificent body was primed for action. 'Perhaps you'll have dinner with me one evening at my home in

Bryonston. I would enjoy the opportunity to introduce you to some of the more modern composers.'

'Perhaps,' she said, not wanting to commit herself one way or the other. 'I'm glad I took your advice, for medical as well as personal reasons. I needed this break away from Courtney's to get things into perspective, and I'm almost ashamed to admit that, after four weeks at Rosslee, Johannesburg seems so far away that it might as well be situated on another continent.'

'That's how it should be, and I envy you the fact that you still have another week here at Rosslee while my holiday has dwindled down to five days.' He captured her glance and smiled twistedly. 'Will you miss me when I'm gone?'

'I shan't miss you at all,' she responded mockingly, but there was a hollow feeling inside her that made a lie of what she had said. 'I'll at last have time to finish that mystery novel I took out of the hotel library more than two weeks ago.'

'You're not very good for my ego, Sarah,' he laughed shortly, the throaty sound scraping across her sensitive nerves, and she shrugged her shoulders with a contrived casualness.

'I'm sorry if you find the truth deflating.'

'I appreciate honesty, especially in women.' He accepted her statement calmly, but Sarah felt as if she had been caught in the act of committing a punishable offence.

Where had the bantering ended and the seriousness begun? She was not sure that she could pin-point the exact moment, but there was one thing which she knew with absolute certainty. It was time to go.

'Stay and have dinner with me this evening,' Anton

invited unexpectedly as if he had tuned into her thoughts, but she shook her head and swallowed down the last mouthful of coffee.

'It will soon be dark, and I must get back to the hotel,' she said, placing her cup on the tray.

'I make a pretty good salad, you know that, and I have enough meat for a *braai*. Am I tempting you?' he asked when she hesitated on the edge of the chair.

'A *braai* is always tempting,' she admitted reluctantly.

'Does that mean you'll stay?'

His blue eyes were narrowed to lazy slits, but Sarah knew him well enough to recognise the deception. Behind those heavy lids his eyes were alert, missing nothing from the nervous flutter of her hands in her lap to the indecision that held her riveted to the edge of her chair. Should she go, or should she stay? He smiled at her; a warm, embracing smile that made her bones feel as if they had turned to jelly, and her resolve weakened.

'I'll stay.' She could not decide whether she should laugh or be angry with him when she saw the look of triumph that flashed across his ruggedly handsome face. 'Are you always this persuasive?' she demanded.

'When I want something badly enough, and I want you, Sarah,' he stated baldly, shaking her to her foundations and confirming her suspicions that she was treading on dangerous ground with Anton.

Stay calm! she warned herself, her fingers digging into the padded edge of the chair in a physical attempt to steady herself. He's trying to provoke you, so for God's sake stay calm!

'You can't have me, Anton.' You wouldn't want me if you knew, she could have added.

'I will have you, Sarah, but only when you're ready,' he drawled with a confidence that sent a thread of panic weaving its way through her.

'I'll never be ready,' she insisted, but she no longer sounded convincing to her own ears, and the glitter of mockery in Anton's eyes told her that he thought the same. 'Let's end this discussion,' she added tersely, wondering if it was too late for her to revert to her decision to leave.

'Don't go away,' he said as if he had sensed her change of mood and, gesturing to her to remain seated, he got up and slid open the glass doors.

The Mozart violin concerto had ended a long time ago, but Sarah only realised it now as her gaze followed Anton out on to the patio where the setting sun was deepening the shadows beneath the scarlet bougain-villaea ranking along the overhead beams. She watched Anton light the fire, and a shutter suddenly clicked in her brain. The barbecue had been stacked and prepared prior to their arrival at the chalet as if Anton had known that the day would end here, and Sarah was suddenly engulfed in a wave of indignation.

Anton was a clever, conniving devil, and a master at getting what he wanted, she realised as she rose agitatedly to her feet. Nothing had been left to chance, everything had been planned, and he had known exactly which strings to pull to get her to co-operate.

'I doubt that you would have had a *braai* on your own, so you must have been pretty sure I would agree to stay when you stacked that fire,' Sarah confronted him when he returned to the lounge.

'I wasn't sure, but I was hoping,' he confessed with a slow smile that did something to the rhythm of her pulse. 'Would you like to help me with the salad?'

Her mouth tightened angrily as she bent down to pick up the tray on the low table between them. She felt like throwing the tray at him, but instead she expelled that desire on an inward sigh of resignation.

'Sure,' she agreed abruptly, following him into the kitchen.

CHAPTER SEVEN

ANTON had decanted a bottle of Cabernet Sauvignon. This was yet another annoying indication of his confidence in himself that he could persuade Sarah to stay, but drinking the full-bodied red wine did help to ease the tension between them while they prepared the salad and spiced the meat in the chalet's small, modern kitchen.

The sun was setting swiftly and casting a pink hue in the cloud-flecked sky when Anton drew the curtains across the kitchen window and switched on the light. He helped himself to a second glass of Cabernet, and leaned back casually against the cupboard behind her with one long, muscular leg crossed over the other. He sipped his wine, watching her in silence while she added the finishing touches to the salad, and Sarah sensed rather than saw his brooding glance following every move she made.

What was he thinking?

'You always project such an ethereal image of cool elegance and sophistication to the media, but I wonder what people would say if they could see this domesticated Sarah Courtney with an apron tied about her waist,' he said as if she had voiced her query.

'You make me sound like a spirit from another world instead of a human being,' she tried to laugh off his remark.

'There is a definite aura of unreality about you, but you're very human, Sarah, and these past two weeks at

Rosslee have made me realise that underneath that cool, aloof exterior you can be warm and giving. Right now I find you very sexy in that apron.'

His voice had deepened with a sensuality that sent a stinging warmth surging into her cheeks, and she could almost resent him for affecting her in this way.

'If you're not careful I might think you make a habit of slapping an apron on the women you invite here to the chalet so that you can tell them they look sexy,' she accused without turning, but she regretted her flippant remark the next instant.

'What makes you think I've had a woman here before?' Anton demanded darkly, forcing her to clarify her statement.

'It was the tennis racket,' she heard herself explaining. 'The grip is too small for it ever to have belonged to a man.'

Her back was turned resolutely towards him, and she held her breath nervously while she chopped up the parsley and sprinkled it over the salad.

'Yes, you're correct in your assumption,' he confirmed calmly after a few tense seconds had elapsed, and Sarah expelled the air slowly from her lungs. 'I bought the tennis racket for a woman I'd invited to accompany me here to Rosslee. I was thinking seriously of settling down at the time, but two weeks here at the chalet with her was enough to make me realise that I'd be making a dreadful mistake if I asked her to marry me.' He was silent for a moment then he asked, 'Do you suppose I'm being too cautious and that I'm wasting the best years of my life?'

Sarah tried to consider this objectively, but her feelings had somehow become entangled in her thoughts. 'That depends on what you want from life.'

'I presume you're trying to tell me that, if I don't speed up my search for the right woman, I might find myself too old to enjoy my children.'

Was that what she had implied? she wondered distractedly. Yes, she supposed it was. But only God would know why she had touched on a subject which would always remain a raw wound inside her.

'That's it exactly,' she said, her throat tightening until her breathing felt restricted, and she prayed Anton would not see the slight tremor in her hands as she rinsed them under the tap and wiped them on a paper towel before untying the apron about her waist. 'I take it you want children?' she prompted with a forced casualness when he remained silent.

'Very much. Doesn't everyone?'

Sarah had expected that, but she was unprepared for the stab of pain that convulsed her insides. She closed her eyes for a moment, willing the self-inflicted pain away, but it was still there even when she had succeeded in controlling her features and, curling her fingers around the stem of her empty glass, she turned to face Anton.

'I think I'd like some more wine.'

'Have I said something wrong?' he asked, quick to notice her unusual pallor while he poured wine into her glass.

'No, you haven't.' Her lowered lashes veiled the pain in her eyes as she raised her glass to her lips, and she gulped down rather a large mouthful of the crimson liquid in an attempt to steady herself. 'Isn't it about time the meat was put on the fire?' she changed the subject, combing her fingers through her shoulder-length hair which had dried naturally after her shower.

'You're right, it's time the meat went on the fire,' he said, glancing briefly at his watch at reaching for the platter containing the T-bone steaks and *boerewors*.

Sarah did not follow him out on to the patio. She lingered in the kitchen to search for salad spoons and to wipe the plates they were going to use. It was a task which could have waited, but she needed to be alone for a few minutes.

Why had it hurt so much when Anton had confirmed that he wanted children? It was only natural that he would want a family of his own one day when he had found the right woman to share his life. So why should it hurt so much to hear him say it?

The answer rose to the surface of her mind with a stunning force that made her sway against the cupboard. *She* wanted to be his woman, *she* wanted to have his children for him, only . . .

Oh, God, why? Haven't I suffered enough? Why did you have to make me feel again . . . want again?

Her hands tightened on the edge of the cupboard until her knuckles whitened. She blamed herself. She had walked into this with her eyes wide open, believing stupidly that she had the situation under control, but she had been sadly mistaken.

Oh, what an *idiot* she had been not to recognise the fact that Anton de Ville had the power to make her care in a way she had never cared before! She had felt the attraction from the start, she had suspected that it could be fatal, but she had allowed herself to be led by her curiosity instead of her common sense.

Sarah knew how to hide her feelings, she had had years of experience in that field, and she was outwardly in complete command of herself when she finally left the kitchen to join Anton out on the well-lit patio where the tempting aroma of meat grilling on the open fire mingled with the sweet fragrance of the night flowers.

The moon was rising high over the ocean, adding a touch of fluorescence to the foamy waves tumbling towards the beach where the wild strelitzias towered like palms on a tropical island. The air was warm and balmy, it was a perfect night for lovers to reach out and find each other, but Sarah knew that for her it was going to be a night of retreat. This was where it had to end —for her sake as well as Anton's.

She could not fault the preparation of the T-bone steaks and spicy sausages, but neither could she enjoy them while her thoughts and her feelings were at war with each other. She knew what she had to do, but her treacherous heart was not in agreement.

'You've been very quiet,' Anton remarked later that evening after they had washed the dishes and were tidying the kitchen.

'You weren't in a very talkative mood yourself,' she replied, wiping the sides of the sink with an unnecessary vigour while the soapy water drained away.

'I've been thinking,' he said.

'So have I.'

'Could it be that we've been thinking the same thing?'

'I doubt it,' she almost snapped at him while she dried her hands on the cloth.

She turned, ready at last to say her piece and leave, but in her agitation she had forgotten that the kitchen space was limited, and the words locked in her throat as she collided unexpectedly with Anton's hard body.

His hands had settled on her waist to steady her, her own lay against his wide chest where she could feel the heavy beat of his heart through the thinness of his white shirt, and her carefully planned speech fled from her mind when she saw her own desire mirrored in his ruggedly handsome face.

This wasn't what she had planned, she thought a little wildly, wanting to push him away, but his hands had already shifted down over her buttocks to draw her up against his aroused body.

'Anton . . . please . . .' she begged huskily, her fingers curling in rejection against his chest and spreading wide again as if her palms could not bear to be parted for one instant from the warmth of his body, and she wondered crazily whether she had actually voiced a plea for release, or a plea for him to continue.

'You have nothing to fear, my lovely Sarah, I'm not going to hurt you.'

Oh, if only you knew, Anton! she wanted to say, but her arms had already circled his neck, and his warm, sensuous mouth had settled on hers, his tongue sliding between her eagerly parted lips to explore the tender moistness within. This was what she wanted, this was what she needed, and nothing else suddenly seemed to matter beyond that achingly sweet fire which had been lit inside her.

Anton's hands roamed her body freely, stroking and coaxing her into a clamouring awareness of a need so intense that she moaned softly against his mouth when his fingers found the hardened peaks of her breasts through the fine cotton of her blouse.

'What are you doing?' she demanded moments later in a startled whisper as he picked her up in his arms and carried her out of the kitchen.

'We'll be more comfortable in the lounge.'

Her tawny eyes widened, conveying her alarm as she raised her glance to that rugged face which was so close to her own. 'Anton, I–I'm not——'

'Hush, my love, you're safe with me,' he interrupted her throatily.

'But I——'

HIs mouth shifted over hers, silencing her effectively, and she felt the muscles knotting across his back as he lowered her gently on to the long, wide sofa and lay down beside her.

'You're safe with me,' he had said. *Safe?* The word echoed hollowly through her mind. She wanted to feel safe and secure and loved, but she could expect none of these things when she had so little to give in return.

Anton's hands gentled her as if he had sensed her mental withdrawal, and his warm mouth trailed a sensually arousing path from her lips to the shadowy, sensitive hollow at the base of her throat before it settled on hers again with a passionate urgency that made her relinquish the effort to think clearly. She wanted him, she wanted the sweet fire of his touch, and that was the only thing that mattered at this moment.

His fingers did not fumble when he undid the buttons of her blouse, and neither did he have difficulty with the front catch of her bra. His mouth left hers when he eased himself away from her slightly to peel aside the strips of lacy satin, exposing the pale, pink-tipped mounds of tender flesh where the sun had not touched her skin, and Sarah drew a ragged breath as his hand gently cupped her breast.

Anton shifted his body over hers, pinning her to the

sofa as he bowed his head over her left breast, and the erotic arousal of his tongue hardened the nipple into an aching pinnacle of desire before he took it into his warm, moist mouth and sucked gently. The shaft of pleasure that shot through her made her body arch beneath his, and her fingers curled convulsively into the dark hair cropped so close to his head, almost guiding his mouth to her other breast where the nipple had hardened in anticipation.

Her excitement mounted sharply when she felt his hand beneath her skirt, trailing upwards along her smooth thigh to her flat stomach, and she wanted him so much at that moment that the quivering tautness in her loins was almost an agony.

'Heaven help me, Sarah, but I want you!' he groaned against her throat, his fingers dipping boldly beneath the flimsy elastic of her panties, and the sound of that deep-throated voice, ragged with desire, brought her swiftly and painfully to her senses.

'Oh, God, no! *No!*' she cried, fear lending a higher pitch to her voice as she struggled beneath him and pushed wildly at the shoulders she had caressed only moments before. 'Let me go!' she begged, terrifyingly close to tears. 'Please! For God's sake, Anton, let me go!'

He released her at once, his breathing laboured and a stunned, slightly incredulous expression on his face as he lowered his feet to the carpeted floor and sat up. A strangled sob escaped Sarah as she scrambled off the sofa to put as much distance as she could between them, and her hands were shaking visibly when she fastened the catch of her bra and buttoned up her blouse.

Anton watched her in silence, taking in the paleness

of her features in the soft glow of the reading lamp, but his sensuous mouth tightened in something close to anger when he glimpsed the sheen of tears in her eyes. 'Sarah?' He rose to his feet, his hands reaching out to her. 'For pity's sake, don't cry, my love.'

'Don't touch me!' she wailed, fighting back those ridiculous tears as she darted away from him with a heart that had not yet resumed its normal pace.

'Did I frighten you?' he demanded softly without attempting to approach her again.

'No.' She lowered her head, looking away, and her hair fell forward like a heavy golden-brown veil to hide her anguished expression.

'I believe you wanted me as much as I wanted you, and if I didn't frighten you, then I must have done something to make you reject me so suddenly,' he reasoned with a quiet calmness she envied at that moment. 'Tell me where I've failed you, Sarah my love.'

I'm the failure, not you! Sarah wanted to shout at him. And I'm not your love, but oh, God how I wish I were!

She regained her equilibrium with difficulty, and her features were composed, though still pale, when she finally raised her glance. 'I don't want to talk about it!' she snapped unnecessarily.

'All right, so we won't talk about it now!' Anton snapped back at her with the first real sign of anger and she turned from him before he could see the film of renewed tears in her eyes.

'I'm sorry, I—I'd better go,' she muttered ruefully, picking up her bag and walking away from him, but he was at the door before her.

'I'll escort you back to the hotel,' he said, and Sarah

nodded her acceptance without looking at him as they stepped out into the night and followed the moonlit path up to the hotel in silence.

Sarah had regretted many things in her life, but the misery her actions had caused her had never been anything quite like this. She should never have allowed her relationship with Anton to progress this far. It had been a mistake from the start, and it was a mistake which she knew she was going to pay for dearly.

'Sarah . . . ' Anton's hand touched her arm briefly to detain her when they reached the steps leading up to the entrance of the hotel, and she turned warily to face him. 'I realise that on such a short acquaintance this might be difficult for you to accept, but I want you to know that you can trust me.'

He spoke with a quiet dignity that touched her more than anything had ever done before, and if she had doubted herself before, then she was convinced now. She loved Anton. She loved him with a depth of feeling which she had never thought herself capable of, but she was still rational enough to recognise the fact that her love for him could lead to her own destruction.

'I do trust you, Anton, but there are certain things . . .'

Her voice faltered precariously, and she looked away, fighting for control before she continued. 'There's been enough pain in my past for me to want to avoid it if I can, and I'm very much afraid that we're only going to hurt each other.'

'Sometimes it's a chance we have to take.'

'Not in this instance,' she contradicted him, and her heart ached when she saw his tight-lipped expression in the shaft of light that spilled out from the hotel foyer across the slate patio and the shallow steps where they stood. 'I think it would be best for both of us if we didn't see each other again.'

'I ought to say "To *hell* with you" and walk away, but I can't, Sarah, and I wish to God I knew why!' he announced with a savage hiss that made her back a nervous pace away from him before she turned and walked briskly up the steps into the well-lit foyer.

She collected her key from the clerk at the reception desk, and when she turned Anton was no longer standing there at the bottom of those shallow slate steps. She should have been relieved that he had gone, but she was not. Her body suddenly felt leaden, and it seemed an effort to drag herself up the stairs to her room.

Sarah neither saw nor heard from Anton during the next two days. Staying away from each other was the sensible thing to do, that was what she had said, but no amount of logical reasoning could erase the hurt, and she wondered eventually if anything ever would.

On the afternoon of the third day, when she was on her way to the lounge to have tea, the desk clerk called her and handed her an envelope with her name printed on it in Anton's bold handwriting. Sarah's heart jolted in her breast and, too distracted at that moment to help herself to a cup of tea, she walked on past the partly empty lounge and out of the building.

There was a strong breeze blowing up from the south. It tugged at the scarf with which she had tied her hair back into the nape of her neck, and it whipped her floral skirt about her legs, but Sarah barely noticed it as she wandered out to the deserted pool area where she opened the envelope with hands that were not quite steady. It contained a single sheet of paper, and on it was written simply, 'I love you, Sarah.'

The message was concise and to the point, and it had come from a man who, in a matter of a few weeks, had got to know her almost better, it seemed, than she knew herself. She might have viewed a florid declaration with disbelief and contempt, but those four words slammed into Sarah's brain with an authenticity that made her reel physically and mentally beneath the impact.

She should have felt elated knowing that Anton loved her, but instead her misery was intensified, and she swayed towards the nearest chair to lower her trembling body into it. Then she did something which she had not done in a very long time. She burst into tears.

That was how Rose Poole found her, sitting hunched on a chair while she wept choking, despairing tears into her hands. Sarah was aware of Rose pulling up a chair and seating herself, but it was a long time before she could control herself sufficiently to wipe her eyes and blow her nose on the wad of tissues which Rose had proffered in solemn silence.

'You've fallen in love with Anton, haven't you?' Rose finally summed up the situation with her usual accuracy, and Sarah felt too drained at that moment to deny it.

'Yes, I have.'

She stared blindly at the crystal-clear water lapping at the edges of the large kidney-shaped pool, and she made a concerted effort to raise herself from that well of misery into which she had slipped as she folded a tissue double and dabbed at the moisture which was still clinging to her puffy eyelids.

'And Anton?' Rose questioned her abruptly.

'He says he feels the same way about me—at least, that's what he's written in this note.' Sarah returned the folded sheet of paper to the envelope and slipped it into her skirt pocket as she added with a wan smile, 'That's what this embarrassing public display is all about.'

Rose raised her shrewd dark eyes from the envelope which Sarah had pushed into her pocket and smiled succinctly. 'When a man puts his feelings on paper it usually means he's serious.'

'That's what I'm afraid of.' Sarah expelled the words on a sigh and lifted a shaky hand to brush a stray strand of hair out of her face.

'When a man says he loves you it doesn't necessarily mean that he wants to marry you,' Rose bounced back. 'You and Anton are two of a kind, you're both seemingly determined to go through life without the commitment marriage requires, so I don't know why this declaration of his should frighten you.'

Sarah shook her head in denial and dabbed hastily at those tears which had risen so readily to her eyes. 'Anton will get married some day when he meets the right woman, he told me so himself.'

'Just as *you* will get married some day when the right man comes along,' Rose stated firmly, voicing her disbelief in Sarah's aversion to marriage. 'I take it you don't consider yourself the right woman for Anton de Ville?'

Sarah swallowed at that aching lump in her throat and shook her head adamantly. 'I *know* I'm not the right woman for him, and I could never marry him even if he should ask me.'

'Because of that deep shadow in your past?'

Rose had touched a raw, exposed nerve, and Sarah

winced and recoiled inwardly from the pain which she knew the older woman had inflicted unintentionally.

'Yes,' she said eventually, seeking a measure of release from that deep-seated anguish in this confession. 'I could never marry Anton—or *any* other man—because of something that happened to me a long time ago.'

'Were you raped?' Rose demanded tersely, jumping to the most obvious conclusion.

'No!' Sarah's eyes had darkened with the pain of remembering as she lifted her head to look at Rose. 'It was nothing like that!'

'Well, if marriage is out of the question, and if having sex with a man isn't an obstacle, then why not settle for an affair with Anton?'

'*Rose!*'

'You're a woman with an above average intelligence, Sarah, so don't look so shocked,' Rose responded with a faintly derisive laugh. 'It's happening all the time, and you know it.'

'Yes, I know, but——'

'You want him, don't you?' Rose cut in with a bluntness which would have penetrated the most strong-minded person's wall of reserve.

'I . . . yes, I . . .' Sarah floundered helplessly, her cheeks flagging with embarrassment.

'If you want him, Sarah, then go ahead and take whatever it is he's offering you.'

Sarah leaned back weakly in her chair. 'But what about afterwards?'

'Let the future take care of itself,' Rose brushed the query aside with an impatient wave of her delicately veined hand, but Sarah could not agree with her.

'What joy is there in becoming emotionally and physically involved with a man when you know it can't last and that the eventual parting is going to bring you pain?'

'All partings are painful, my dear Sarah, but you will at least have stored up a collection of happy memories to sustain you.'

'Oh, Rose!' Sarah sighed with a mirthless smile curving her generous mouth. 'You make it all sound so simple, but we both know it isn't.'

'Life is never simple, my dear,' Rose assured her gravely, 'but sometimes we're driven to take what we can get in order to go on living.'

Sarah lapsed into a thoughtful silence as she stared at the fragile little woman with the snow-white hair plaited and coiled neatly about her head. Rose Poole was speaking from experience, there was a look of remembered happiness and pain in those dark eyes, and Sarah had to admit that there was a certain logic in the advice Rose had given, but she was too rigidly principled to accept it.

'I'm going for a walk,' she announced a few minutes later, rising to her feet and disposing of the bundle of soggy tissues in the nearest bin.

'Don't walk too far,' Rose warned solicitously, glancing up at the sky. 'There's a heavy bank of storm-clouds shifting up from the south, and we can expect a downpour before dark.'

Sarah had had every intention of heeding Rose's warning when she followed one of the well-trodden paths along the rugged coastline, but she had been so engrossed in her own turbulent thoughts that she had walked much further than she had intended. The wind had reached gale-force momentum and the sky was darkening ominously when she seated herself tiredly on a patch of wild grass to read Anton's note once again.

'I love you, Sarah.'

The wind tore at the sheet of paper in her hands, almost ripping it from her grasp, and stinging, desolate tears filled her eyes and spilled from her lashes to roll unheeded down her cheeks as she folded the letter and returned it to her pocket for safe keeping.

'Oh, Anton!' His name passed her lips in an agonised cry which was lost in the wind when she drew her legs up against her and lowered her head to her knees. 'Anton! Anton!'

Sarah was too busy drowning in her own sorrowful thoughts to see the first flash of lightning fork across the blackened sky, and neither had she been aware of that first angry rumble of thunder which had made the earth shudder beneath her. It was the stinging, wind-driven force of those first heavy drops of rain that brought her smartly to her senses. She leapt to her feet, cursing herself silently for not having paid more attention to the weather, and moments later she was caught up at the very centre of a frightening downpour which soaked her to the skin in seconds.

She glanced about her a little wildly. There was nowhere she could go for cover, and it was suddenly so dark that she knew she would have difficulty following the path back to the hotel, but that was the only thing left for her to do.

Fifteen minutes later she was beginning to fear that she had wandered off in the wrong direction, and then, when a flash of lightning tore across the sky with a deafening crack that shook the earth, she saw the cluster

of tall, jagged rocks where the path split in two. The one
path led to the hotel, and the other to the chalets.

The rain was lashing her mercilessly, and she was
frozen to such an extent that her teeth were chattering,
but she could not move away from that spot. She had
literally and figuratively reached the crossroads where
the two paths joined, looking at that moment like
miniature rivers flowing into one. The water was
gushing over her feet, ruining her expensive sandals, but
she stood leaning against the jagged rocks as if she had
suddenly become a solidified part of that particular
piece of petrified nature.

She was recalling her conversation with Rose and she
was remembering in frightening detail what the shrewd
old lady had said to her. Sarah tried to slam a mental
door on the memory, but Rose's words invaded her mind
with the persistence of a toothache which refused to be
ignored.

'If you want him, then go ahead and take whatever it
is he's offering you . . . sometimes we're driven to take
what we can get in order to go on living.'

'Oh, God, help me! *Please,* help me!' Sarah prayed
out loud, closing her eyes against the rain battering her
face and her body when she felt herself drowning in an
aching surge of longing. 'I want him and I don't know
what to do about it. Oh, God, *please!*'

She tried to clear her mind of everything, but one
word remained like the sting of a bee.

Driven!

Rose had said, 'Sometimes we're *driven* to take what
we can get in order to go on living', and that was how
Sarah felt at that moment. She started walking, blinded
by the tears which mingled with the rain on her face,

and she went on walking until she saw the lights of Anton's chalet up ahead through the madly waving trees and wild strelitzias. She did not want to go there, but she also knew that she *had* to.

Minutes later she was standing beneath the shelter of the balcony at the entrance to the chalet. Her clothes were clinging to her like a second skin, and the water was dripping down along her shivering body to collect in a puddle at her feet when the door was wrenched open in answer to her ring. Anton stared at her for a moment as if she were an apparition, then an angry oath escaped him as he dragged her inside and slammed the door against the raging elements outside.

'Are you trying to catch your death walking around in this filthy weather?' he demanded harshly, flicking a clinical glance over her wet, shivering body, and Sarah's teeth were chattering so much that she had difficulty in answering him.

'I w-went for a w-walk, and I—'

'Later!' he interrupted her sharply, sweeping her up into his arms as if she weighed no more than a child, and striding towards the stairs. 'You can tell me later!'

CHAPTER EIGHT

THE bath had been filled almost to the rim, and Sarah had no conception of time as she lay soaking in the hot water, listening to the storm raging overhead while the icy coldness was being driven from her body.

She had been so frozen when Anton had carried her up to his bedroom and into his blue and white tiled bathroom that her fingers had refused to carry out his instruction that she take off her clothes while he ran the bathwater. In the end he had been forced to help her strip the wet things from her shivering body, and Sarah had been too numb with the cold at that moment to be anything but grateful.

It was now, with the warmth flowing rapidly back into her body, that she felt a twinge of embarrassment at the memory of how he had divested her of her saturated clothes until she had stood naked before him, but he had not lingered in the bathroom after performing that duty. He had stayed only to tell her that she could wear the white robe which hung on the hook behind the door, and then he had left, taking her bundle of wet clothes with him to put them in the tumble drier.

Sarah dried herself quickly when she finally got out of the bath, and her skin was tingling with warmth as she lifted Anton's short towelling robe off the hook. She slipped her arms into the sleeves, and had to suppress the desire to laugh out loud when she wrapped it about herself and studied her image in the mirrored wall. The hem of the robe hung down about her ankles, the armhole seams of the sleeves sat halfway between her shoulders and her elbows, and the wide cuffs of the three-quarter-length sleeves reached down to her wrists.

She knotted the belt firmly about her waist, convinced that she looked a dishevelled sight, but the towelling material was warm, and that was all that mattered, she decided sensibly as she removed the small towel which she had wrapped haphazardly about her head before she had got into the bath. Her hair had dried considerably, but she gave it a vigorous rub with the towel for good measure, and combed it into a certain amount of order with her fingers before she left the bathroom.

Sarah stopped short as she entered the brightly lit bedroom to see Anton putting something on the circular table beside the burgundy red curtains which had been drawn across the sliding doors that led out on to the balcony.

He straightened and turned, his clinical, appraising glance sweeping her from her damp, untidy hair down to her bare toes curling into the soft carpet beneath her feet. Sarah studied him just as closely, and if she had expected him to look any different, then she was disappointed. There was nothing in his expression to give her any indication as to his feelings, and she wondered if it was possible that she could have imagined the words he had written on that sheet of paper which was now being dried in the tumble drier along with the rest of her clothes.

Anton was still wearing his slip-on canvas shoes and grey denim trousers, but he had exchanged the white shirt she had dampened for a blue one which he had left unbuttoned and hanging loosely over the broad leather belt that hugged his trousers to his lean hips. It added a touch of wildness to that aura of raw masculinity he always exuded, and Sarah averted her gaze nervously from that shadow of body hair trailing down to his navel, focusing her attention instead on the table, which had been laid for two.

'It's curried stew and rice,' he explained, following the direction of her gaze. 'The Indian cleaning lady prepared it earlier today and left it in the oven for this evening, but, as usual, it's too much for me to eat on my own.'

The thought of food did not appeal to her at that moment. 'I'm not hungry.'

'Come,' he said bluntly, ignoring her statement and walking round the table to pull a chair for her. 'Sit here and don't argue,' he added crisply.

The last thing Sarah wanted to do was to argue with him. She felt pleasantly relaxed despite that feeling of nervous anticipation spiralling through her, but she was very much aware of Anton's eyes observing her with a strange intensity in their depths when she stepped past the enormous bed with its burgundy and white striped duvet and heavily padded headboard.

Anton pushed her chair in for her and spooned rice and curried stew into their plates before he seated himself opposite her. The table was small, if she altered her position slightly their knees might touch, and Sarah's hands trembled visibly as she picked up her knife and fork. She had not been hungry, but after the first mouthful of food she discovered that she was ravenous, and she was glad that Anton had been so insistent.

The storm passed while they ate their meal and,

except for the occasional rumble of thunder which was still strong enough to make the building shudder beneath them, the worst was over.

'Feeling better?' Anton questioned her some time later with a faint smile relieving the severity of his expression as he slid her empty plate into his.

'Much better, thank you.' She dabbed at her lips with a paper serviette and leaned back in her chair with a satisfied sigh.

'You may give your cleaning lady my compliments. The curried stew was excellent.'

'Stay where you are,' he instructed, piling the dishes on to a tray. 'I'll bring us a mug of coffee.'

Sarah rose from her chair to wander about the room when she was alone and the leather suitcase beside the dressing-table, packed and ready for his departure in the morning, did not escape her notice. It enhanced that restless, almost agitated feeling inside her when she combed her tangled hair away from her face with her fingers to take a critical look at herself in the dressing-table mirror, but it was the reflected image of the bed behind her which caught and held her attention.

Anton had made love on that bed with another woman. Sarah had no right to be jealous, but she was. She passed a shaky hand over her eyes and walked away from that reflected image in the mirror to draw the curtain aside.

She had no right to be jealous of the women who had preceded her in Anton's life, she reasoned with herself as she stared out into the inky blackness beyond the glass doors where a periodic flash of lightning still lit up the sky in the distance. Anton was, after all, not the first man in *her* life. There had been Nigel. Nigel who had subjected her to his morally annihilating accusations when the accident had left her emotionally cold and physically empty.

Her fingers curled into her palms until her nails bit sharply into her flesh. She did not want to think about Nigel. Not tonight of all nights. The next few hours were still a mystery to her and, regardless of what might evolve from it, she wanted this night to belong solely to Anton and herself. No one else must be allowed to intrude, not even in thought.

Sarah released the curtain to let it fall back into place as Anton entered the room a few minutes later, and she felt strangely calm as she watched him place two steaming mugs of coffee on the table.

'Rose phoned earlier while you were in the bath,' he informed her while he dimmed the lights in the room down to the bedside lamps.

'Poor Rose!' A rueful sigh escaped Sarah as she resumed her seat at the table. 'I imagine she must have been worried.'

'She was in quite a state, but I managed to assure her that you had turned up dripping but unharmed on my doorstep.'

A wall of silence settled between them while they sat at the table drinking their coffee, and it was a silence filled with an understandable tension. They both knew they had some explaining to do, but they were both equally reluctant to make that first vital move. Sarah searched for something to say, *anything* which might ease the tension between them, but her mind remained a stubborn blank, and it was Anton who finally broached the subject which was foremost in their minds.

'Would you mind explaining to me what you were

doing out in the storm?' he demanded with a certain harshness in his voice when he set aside his empty mug.

'I received your note this afternoon.' She realised at once that she had leapt foolishly into the centre of the verbal arena with that statement, but it was too late now to retract it as she felt her heart being wrenched at the sight of Anton's twisted, faintly cynical smile.

'Did you find the contents of my note so distasteful that you had to rush off and wander blindly into one of the worst storms I believe we've had in a long time here at the coast?' he demanded once again, the harshness in his voice deepening, and Sarah could not control the tremor in her hand as she deposited her mug on the table.

'It wasn't that,' she corrected him as she clasped her hands nervously in her lap. 'I——I knew there was a storm approaching, Rose had warned me about it, but I had so much to——to think about and I——I'm afraid I didn't notice the weather until it was too late.' She was stammering with a lack of confidence which belonged to her insecure youth, and she hated herself for it as she rose agitatedly to her feet and wrapped her arms protectively about herself. 'It wasn't my intention to come here, Anton,' she added, determined to tell him the truth, but not daring to look at him while she did so. 'I didn't *want* to come here, but in the end I . . . I *had* to.'

'Why?' Anton had come up behind her so silently that she had not heard him, but his hands were surprisingly gentle when he took her by the shoulders and turned her to face him. 'Why did you have to come?'

'I'm so tired of running away from my feelings, and I——' She gestured helplessly with her hands, overwhelmed suddenly by his nearness and that helpless longing which she no longer had the strength to suppress. 'What do you really want of me, Anton?' she asked with a catch of uncertainty in her husky voice, and his expression softened miraculously.

'I want to love you, Sarah,' he said quietly, his eyes warm and deeply probing as he slid his hands down her back to draw her up against him, and she felt herself melting against that barrier of taut muscles and heated maleness.

'I want that too,' she confessed shakily, her eyes misting with emotion and her hands finding a resting place against his chest where she could feel the strong, rhythmic thudding of his heart through his shirt.

'I not only want to love you, Sarah, I want it to be perfect for both of us, but if you're not——'

'It *will* be perfect,' she interrupted hastily, silencing him with her fingers against his lips. 'I know it . . . I feel it.'

That was the truth, she was thinking moments later when his mouth brushed lightly against her closed eyelids before trailing a tantalising path of feather-light kisses down to her eagerly parted lips. There was a pulsating warmth deep down inside her, and a longing which no logic could assuage. In the cold light of day she might consider it wrong, but at that moment it all seemed so right. She wanted Anton; she wanted him as she had never wanted any other man before, and that was all that mattered at that moment.

Her hands found their way inside his shirt, her palms loving the feel of his warm, hair-roughened skin as she explored his muscled chest, and the sharp intake of his breath did not escape her when the tips of her fingers brushed lightly against his hard male nipples.

Anton's arousal was swift and strong, thrusting against her through the barrier of their clothes, and there was a distinct thrill in the discovery that she could have this power to stir him physically.

'Slowly, Sarah.' His throaty warning against her mouth stayed the action of her hands. 'I want you so much that I could have you now, but then it wouldn't be perfect for you, so don't rush it, my love.'

Sarah felt like a novice, and she soon discovered how much of a novice she was when Anton proceeded to initiate her into the true art of making love. She sensed very quickly that this was not going to be a selfish, one-sided affair, but an encounter of a very different kind which would be aimed at their mutual satisfaction, and, with that in mind, she was perfectly willing to follow where Anton led.

His hands roamed her body, igniting a fire of their own while they acquainted themselves with the hollows and curves of her feminine structure beneath the towelling robe, but it was his sensually erotic kisses which succeeded in arousing her senses to a pitch of almost feverish delight. Her body swayed against his, yielding against the hardness of his muscle-toned frame, and her hands shifted up across his broad back to grip his shoulders when he lifted her hair away from her face to expose her slender, arched throat to the exploration of his mouth.

Shivers of pleasure cascaded through her as his tongue flicked across her smooth skin and lingered at sensitive areas which she had not known existed, and she was sinking into a well of the most exquisite sensations when his mouth sought hers again with a searing passion that stripped her mind of everything except the desire to get closer to him.

A whimpering protest spilled from her lips when Anton finally eased himself away from her, but his smouldering eyes held hers captive in the soft light while he shrugged himself out of his shirt and flung it away from him. He kicked off his slip-on canvas shoes and raised his hands to the broad leather belt threaded through the loops of his grey denims. His fingers touched the ornate silver buckle, but they remained there, unmoving, and Sarah knew instinctively what he was waiting for. He wanted a signal; a sign that she was willing to go on. After this, she knew, there would be no turning back, and there had to be no regrets.

She lifted her hands to the towelling belt, tugging at the end of the makeshift bow, and Anton's massive chest heaved as if he had held his breath while he had waited.

They undressed themselves in silence, Anton divesting himself of the remainder of his clothes while Sarah allowed the robe to slide in a slow, unconsciously seductive movement from her shoulders to the carpeted floor, and Anton drew an audible breath when they stood with nothing but the cool night air between them. A muscle leapt in his strong jaw, and there was naked desire in the eyes that left hers to acquaint themselves with her naked body.

'God, but you're beautiful, Sarah!' he groaned softly, his smouldering eyes roaming over her once again in a slow caress that made her skin tingle and burn as if he had actually touched her.

He was beautiful too, she thought as she allowed her glance to wander unashamedly over his aroused, magnificently proportioned body. His broad, muscled chest tapered down to a taut, flat stomach, and there was a strip of white skin across his lean hips where his bathing briefs had prevented the sun from touching his skin.

His hand reached out for Sarah's to lead her towards the bed, and she had no qualms about letting him do so. He drew back the duvet with his free hand, then he lifted her high in his arms and lowered her gently on to the bed. He hovered over her, a hand pressing into the mattress on either side of her body and his biceps bulging as his arms took the weight of his body. His eyes held hers for a moment as if to assure himself of her willingness, then he lay down beside her, their legs entwining as he gathered her into the hard curve of his body and set his mouth on hers with a passionate urgency that made the blood flow faster through her veins.

The feel of his muscled, heated flesh against her own inflamed her, and the feather-light caress of his hands on her body sensitised her skin and awakened a thousand little nerves to the pleasure of his touch. Her slender frame arched against his of its own volition like a cat responding to the loving caress of its owner, and Anton dragged his mouth from hers to straddle her body and bury his face between her breasts with a smothered groan on his lips.

Sarah stiffened beneath him, her teeth sinking into her lower lip to bite back a protest when the old fear returned with a chilling force that robbed her of the emotions he had aroused, but Anton was not an insensitive lover, and her withdrawal did not go unnoticed.

'Relax, Sarah, I'm not going to hurt you,' he murmured, the roughness of his jaw scraping against her breasts when he moved his head. 'Trust me, my love.'

His tongue flicked across one rosy nipple, teasing it into a hard nodule before he took it into his warm mouth and sucked gently. Fear and tension made way for a renewed shaft of pleasure, and her fingers curled almost convulsively into his hair when his mouth shifted to her other breast to repeat the arousing caress.

Anton was a patient lover. His own desire was firmly under control while his hands gentled her and paved the way for the erotic caress of his tongue until it seemed as if every nerve and sinew in her body was shatteringly alive to his touch.

It eventually became virtually impossible for Sarah to think coherently as she felt herself being reduced to a trembling mass of sensations beneath the sensual exploration of his mouth as it trailed over every inch of her body. Every flick of his tongue against her heated, sensitised flesh raised her to a new level of excitement, and she was caught up in a frenzy of the most incredible desire when his mouth finally made its way up along the softness of her quivering inner thigh in search of the most vital part of her womanhood.

Shock mingled with embarrassment, but it was no more than a fleeting sensation. The intimate exploration of Anton's tongue was a fiery delight that drove Sarah to the very edge of desire, and she seemed to hover there, suspended over that unfamiliar portal to pleasure until she was mindless with the driving need to be possessed. Her hips moved as if with a knowledge of their own, making primitive, thrusting movements to convey her need, and she was almost demented with desire when Anton drew himself up between her thighs until his laboured breath mingled with hers.

'Touch me now, Sarah,' he growled impatiently. 'Touch me now.'

His eyes were no longer blue, they were black pinpoints of desire while he supported himself on one elbow to take Sarah's hand and place it flat against his hard, hair-roughened chest. She could feel his heart beating as hard and fast as her own, and then he was guiding her hand down along his body towards his taut, flat stomach.

'Oh, Sarah . . . Sarah!' he groaned, subjecting her to the passionate scrutiny of his glance when she followed the action through until her fingers encountered his heated arousal. 'I feel as if I've waited all my life for this moment,' he added in a voice that was rough and ragged with emotion.

Sarah wanted to say, 'I've waited as well. Oh, *how* I've waited!' but the words remained locked in her throat when Anton's hand slid beneath her buttocks to lift her for his penetration. Her arms went up and around him to draw him closer, and a rapturous sigh escaped her as he entered the cushioned warmth of her body in one long, hard thrust.

She loved him so much, and her feelings were so intense at that moment that she wanted to weep as she buried her face against the hollow of his shoulder and tasted the saltiness of his skin on her tongue. She was impatient for him, everything inside her was crying out for something which she still had no knowledge of, but Anton held her as if he wanted to take a moment to savour his possession of her, and then, with the slow, rhythmic thrust of his hips, he began to arouse sensations of a different kind which sent a shaft of melting fire darting through her veins.

Her pleasure mounted with every quickening thrust of his body until that achingly sweet tension inside her took complete control of her mind, dictating her actions, and her hips rose to meet his, again and again, in that age-old rhythm of love until she was blind and deaf to everything except the exciting smell of him, the taste of his skin on her tongue and the feel of him inside her.

Her breath was coming in little gasps, her fingers digging into Anton's shoulders where the muscles knotted beneath the smooth dampness of his skin, and she locked her legs about his hard thighs in a wild frenzy of excitement as she felt herself being swept towards a peak of near intolerable pleasure.

She had become a willing prisoner of that white-hot blaze of passionate desire, every fibre of her being straining and clamouring towards release as that delicious tension mounted to breaking-point inside her, and she was almost sobbing with the extent of her emotions when their thrashing bodies finally came together in a shattering climax that left her limp and gasping for breath beneath the shuddering weight of Anton's body.

A wave of the most exquisite sensations spiralled through her, and then it ebbed slowly, to leave her tingling from her head down to her toes. The words 'I love you!' came so close to spilling from her lips that she dragged them back forcibly on a choked cry, only to hear Anton's throaty voice murmuring her name over and over again almost as if it were a benediction.

Sarah was filled with awe while they lay with their bodies still locked together and their hearts pounding in the aftermath of their lovemaking. Anton had dispelled her fears. He had reduced her belief that she was sexually inadequate to the proportions of a myth, and she knew she would always be eternally grateful to him for that.

Her happiness was intense. She felt like a woman at last, fulfilled and content in her lover's arms for the first time in her life, but reality had a nasty way of intruding when it was not wanted. She had taken something which would never belong solely to her. She had given herself in return, but in the process she had also made a gift of her heart, and that was something she could never take back. Her eyes filled with tears, and Anton chose that moment to ease himself away from her.

'Why are you crying?' he demanded softly, the perspiration glistening on his body in the soft light as he leaned over her to catch her tears on his tongue before brushing his lips across one flushed cheek in search of her mouth.

'I never thought—it could be—like this,' Sarah whispered shakily in between kisses, hiding her secret knowledge behind a statement of fact as she caressed his shoulders where, in the throes of passion, her fingernails had raked across the skin to leave inflamed weals in their wake.

'Was it as perfect for you as it was for me, my love?' he demanded at length, raising his head to pin her down with his piercing, probing glance.

'Oh, Anton . . . Anton!' His name spilled almost reverently from her lips, and her tawny eyes were luminous with unshed tears as she raised her hand to brush that stubborn curl away from his damp forehead with the tips of her fingers. 'It surpassed all my wildest expectations!'

'I'm glad,' he smiled, capturing her hand in his and pressing his warm mouth into her palm before he relieved her of the weight of his body to pull the duvet over them.

Sarah snuggled up to Anton when they had switched off the lights, and she lay quietly in his arms with her head on his shoulder. Words were unnecessary at that moment, and she wanted to savour every second of this night with him because she knew it would be her last.

Anton seemed equally loath to speak. He was troubled about something, she sensed it in the absent caress of his hands on her body, and she also had a feeling that she knew what could be occupying his thoughts, but she did not want to dwell on it.

'Let the future take care of itself,' Rose had said, and at that moment Sarah was in complete agreement with her elderly friend. This was *now*, and tomorrow was still very much in the future.

'You're not going back to the hotel tonight.' Anton intruded on her thoughts with an unfamiliar urgency in his deep, velvety voice. 'You're staying here with me.'

'What will the hotel staff think when they see my bed hasn't been slept in?' she teased, turning her face into his shoulder and trailing a path of passionate little kisses along his collarbone to the hollow of his throat.

'To hell with what they may think!' he growled, prying her face out into the open and kissing her hard and satisfyingly on the lips. 'You belong here,' he added roughly, 'and this is where you're going to stay.'

Yes, she belonged here, and this was where she was going to stay. For tonight, anyway. Tomorrow was the future, and then the dream of belonging must end.

Anton's arms tightened about her, and his mouth was

hard and demanding when it claimed hers in the darkness. It was as if he had sensed the trend of her thoughts, and Sarah emptied her mind of everything except the joy of this moment.

One kiss led to another in the dark intimacy of the room, their hands touching and stroking until a new hunger erupted between them. It grew fierce and strong, like a fire raging out of control, and they made love this time with a passionate, almost savage urgency which left them spent and physically sated.

Anton went to sleep almost immediately while Sarah tried to fight off that pleasant drowsiness that enveloped her. She did not want to go to sleep, but in the end she did.

She was dreaming. She was young and whole again, unscarred physically and mentally, and she was running across the dunes to where Anton stood waiting for her, but the loose sand retarded her progress. His arms had opened wide, willing her to come to him, and then there was Nigel. Nigel who stood like an impenetrable barrier between Anton and herself, and his harsh, jeering laugh robbed her cruelly of her youth and her dreams. 'You're worthless . . . worthless . . . worthless!' Nigel's accusing voice echoed repeatedly across the dunes. 'No man will want you . . . want you . . . want you!'

Sarah awoke with a start, her heart pounding in her chest and her body clammy. She lay for a moment, waiting for that feeling of relief in knowing that it had only been a dream, but the dream became a nightmare as she faced the reality.

She slipped out of bed and, taking care not to wake Anton, found the towelling robe she had discarded earlier that evening and put it on. It was not cold, but she was shivering, and she tied the belt firmly about her waist as she walked towards the glass doors to draw aside the curtains.

The storm had passed long ago and the sky had cleared except for a fleecy cloud which still hovered like a shadow across the moon. A shadow! There had been too many shadows! Most of them had gone, but one painful truth still remained to cast an eternal shadow over her life.

The thought of Nigel had never failed to conjure up a feeling of inadequacy in the past, but when she thought of him now it was with a glimmer of understanding mingling with her contempt. Mild enjoyment was all she had ever experienced with Nigel, and after the accident his insensitivity had robbed her of even that. She could understand his frustration at her lack of response, but she could never forgive those humiliating accusations which had almost succeeded in ruining her emotionally for the rest of her life.

She wished . . . oh, how she wished it could have been Anton she had met all those years ago instead of Nigel, but the futility of that wish made her eyes fill with anguished tears. She stifled the sob that rose in her throat, and leaned against the steel frame of the sliding door to press her hot forehead against the cool glass while she fought to control herself.

'Sarah?' The sound of Anton's voice startled her, and she spun round without thinking just as he snapped on the bedside light.

'I'm sorry,' she apologised unsteadily, blinking into the soft light until her eyes became accustomed to it. 'I didn't mean to wake you.'

Anton sat up in bed, the muscles rippling in his

shoulders and across his chest when he moved. His gaze was narrowed and intent, and she hastily averted her glance, but not before he had seen the sheen of tears which she had not had time to hide.

'You've been crying,' he accused.

'You see too much,' she retaliated, attempting to laugh and make a joke of it, but her laugh ended in something like a hiccup that made Anton swear under his breath.

'Come here,' he commanded softly but authoritatively, and she found herself obeying. He framed her face in his hands when she was seated on the edge of the bed beside him, and gently brushed the tears from her cheeks with his thumbs. 'Am I the cause of these tears?'

'No.' She curled her fingers about his strong, lean wrists and turned her face into his palms, kissing first the one and then the other. 'I was thinking back over my life,' she explained, the husky quality in her voice deepening with emotion. 'I was wishing I could have known then what I know now.'

Anton's expression remained inscrutable, but his hands fell away from her as he leaned back against the padded headboard and dragged a pillow up behind him for comfort.

'Do you want to tell me about it?' he asked, his head beyond the soft pool of light from the bedside lamp and his features partly in shadow.

Sarah shivered inside the robe as if someone had trickled iced water down her back. It felt as if Anton had not only withdrawn from her physically, but mentally as well, and the agony of it was like a blade to her heart.

CHAPTER NINE

THE night was so quiet that Sarah wondered if Anton could hear the painful beating of her heart while she searched his ruggedly handsome face in the hope of finding something there which might comfort her, but she searched in vain. He had the look of a remote stranger instead of the man she had made passionate love with only a few hours ago, and she was not quite sure how to interpret this change in him.

'You were thinking about your late husband, weren't you?' he prompted questioningly when Sarah remained silent, and his uncanny ability to sense her thoughts and feelings no longer shocked her.

'Yes, I was.' She felt guilty, but she sustained his glance, knowing that there was no sense in hiding the truth from him.

'Tell me about it.'

It was not a query this time, it was an instruction, and Sarah shook her head and looked away nervously. 'This doesn't seem like the right moment to rake up the past and the memory of a man who's been dead for more than six years.'

'You've already done the raking, Sarah,' he observed quietly. 'If there's something in your past that's lying there in your mind like a pile of unsightly leaves, then I'd like to help you dispose of it, and the sooner it's done the better for both of us.'

His description was apt. The past was lying in her mind like a pile of unsightly leaves, and perhaps now *was* the right time to rid herself of that part which could be disposed of. Anton did, at least, deserve an explanation.

'May I let in some air?' she asked, her nervousness driving her on to her feet and across the room to the glass doors.

'Go ahead,' he said, and Sarah slid the door back a short distance.

The stars were out, and a cool breeze drifted into the room bringing with it the sound of the sea and the fragrant scent of the night flowers growing so abundantly below the bedroom balcony. Sarah inhaled their scent, but her mind leapt about frantically, searching for a place to start her tale and not quite finding it. Anton had said he would like to help her, but this was something she had to do on her own.

'I don't quite know where to begin,' she confessed, standing with her back to him while she stared blindly out into the darkness beyond the glass door, but she drew a deep, steadying breath and somehow found the courage to speak about the things which had been locked away inside her for so long. 'Nigel Kemp was very much like my father, and that was perhaps what had attracted me to him in the first place. I was also very immature and vulnerable at the age of nineteen, and I fell for his flattery, but we were scarcely married when I discovered that Nigel cared for me even less than I cared for him. He'd used me to secure his position as my father's successor at Courtney's, and he made no secret of that fact whenever I displeased him.'

Sarah pushed her hands into the wide pockets of Anton's robe and she clenched them so tightly that her nails bit into her soft palms. Anger and bitterness rose like gall into her mouth as she recalled the past, but this time it was directed at herself. She had always blamed everyone except herself for what had happened, but the blame was equally hers. If she had not been so obsessed about gaining her father's love and approval she might have been more aware of what was going on around her. The signs had all been there, but she had been too blind to see them.

'Our marriage was an absolute disaster from the start,' she continued, the memories like acid on her tongue, sharp and stinging. 'Nigel was an insensitive lover. Perhaps if we'd loved each other things might have been different, but under the circumstances I—I always failed to—to respond beyond a certain point. It never stopped Nigel from satisfying his own needs, and I simply took it for granted that that was what—what sex was all about.' Her voice had faltered, fading to a whisper as she related, for the first time, these intimate and painfully embarrassing details, but she cleared her throat and forced herself to go on. 'I was involved in an accident three months after we were married. I was knocked down by a car and—and after that I—I was emotionally frozen. One night when Nigel made—made love to me and I—I couldn't—didn't respond, he—he accused me of being worthless as a woman and of no use to any man.'

The ensuing silence was long and strained before Anton asked, 'Did you mention any of this to your father?'

'I told him that Nigel had married me solely to further his career, but my father wouldn't believe me.' Sarah turned, her face pale and a cynical smile curving her soft mouth as she combed the heavy strands of hair away from her face with agitated fingers. 'He accused me of being hypersensitive like most new brides and of over-reacting like a typical woman. He said he had no intention of involving himself in our marital squabbles, and he more or less accused me of attempting to ruin the good personal and working relationship between Nigel and himself.'

'Why didn't you divorce Nigel?'

'To divorce him would have meant humiliating myself publicly—and believe me, Nigel would have seen to that. Besides . . .' her eyes were almost feverishly bright in the soft light as she searched Anton's shadowy features in a futile attempt to gauge his reaction '. . . our marriage lasted five months, and it disintegrated naturally when Nigel moved out of our suite into another and started living his life apart from mine.'

Anton's mask slipped for the first time to display an element of anger in the tightening of his mouth. 'Didn't your father question Nigel's behaviour?'

'He did.' Sarah smiled derisively. 'But, as always, Nigel had a glib answer ready.'

'I'm giving Sarah time to adjust physically and emotionally to the knowledge that she's lost our child and can't have another.' That was what Nigel had said to Edmond Courtney, and Edmond had believed him. The subject had never been mentioned again, but Sarah had not been blind to the scornful glances her father had directed at her.

'You're an embarrassment to me,' her father had told her shortly before his and Nigel's untimely deaths. 'If your husband is seeking solace in the arms of other women, then you have only yourself to blame for that.'

Sarah had known about Nigel's affairs. He had been very discreet, taking care not to arouse Edmond Courtney's displeasure, but to Sarah he had made no secret of the fact that he was seeing other women. At first it had hurt and humiliated her, but eventually she had simply found it sickening.

Anton sat up in bed, the movement capturing her attention and forcing her to drag her thoughts painfully back to the present as she encountered his piercing, probing glance. He was waiting as if he had sensed that there was more to come, and there was.

'I've believed all these years that I—that I'm frigid.' Her eyes filled with tears as she divulged that information, but her glance did not waver from his when she crossed the room to crawl on to her side of the bed. She sat back on her heels, facing him, and raised her hands in a vaguely imploring gesture. 'During these past weeks you've made me realise that I'm not the cold slab I've always believed myself to be, but I think a part of me feared it and still believed it when I arrived here out of the storm, and then it—it suddenly didn't seem to matter any more.'

'So this is what you were afraid of the other night!' His expression softened with understanding. 'You didn't trust the strength of your own feelings.'

'No, I didn't,' she croaked. 'I was afraid to trust the feelings you were arousing. I was afraid they wouldn't last.'

Anton reached for her, his arms hard about her body as he pulled her down to him until she lay cradled against his wide chest. He held her without speaking, combing his fingers soothingly through her hair and kissing away her tears with a tenderness that made her heart ache with love for him.

'I wish you weren't leaving tomorrow,' she murmured with a new-found confidence, sliding her arms about him and turning her face into his shoulder to explore his collarbone with her tongue.

'I wish I could take you with me,' he groaned, the stubble on his jaw scraping against her temple as he untied the belt about her waist to gain access to her body.

'I could always cancel my flight arrangements for next week and drive back to Johannesburg with you tomorrow,' she volunteered, trembling beneath the light, sensually arousing touch of that warm hand trailing from her throat to her smooth shoulder before it ventured lower to cup her breast.

'It's a tempting thought, but as your doctor I absolutely forbid it,' he said, dashing her hopes sternly while his thumb moved back and forth across her hardened nipple in a tantalising caress. 'I have it on record that I prescribed a minimum of six weeks away from anything and everything connected with Courtney's, and I must insist that you don't alter your arrangements.'

'If I go back with you it doesn't necessarily mean that I'll return to the office before I'm supposed to,' she argued, her lips against his strong throat and her hand moving across his hair-roughened chest in an answering caress.

'Can you see yourself in Johannesburg for a week without getting yourself involved in the activities at Courtney's?'

'No, I can't,' she admitted reluctantly, but truthfully, a slumberous look in her tawny eyes as she raised her face to his, and yet another truth spilled unrehearsed from her quivering lips. 'I'm going to miss you.'

'Are you?' he demanded throatily, his breath mingling with hers while his hand strayed possessively down to her flat stomach.

'Yes! Oh, yes, Anton, I——' His hand slid between her thighs, cutting off what might have been a revealing statement, and she clung to him with a new urgency. 'Make love to me,' she begged huskily, her fingers locked in his hair as she urged his mouth down to hers. 'Please make love to me, Anton.'

'I intend to do just that,' he assured her thickly, his mouth closing over hers and demanding a response which Sarah was only too willing to give.

It was a long time before they were finally able to settle down for the night, and even then it was as if they could not bear to be parted. They went to sleep in each other's arms, their legs entwined, and this time Sarah did not stir until the following morning.

The sun was streaming into the bedroom through the gap in the curtains when she stretched lazily beneath the duvet, and she was vaguely disconcerted until she remembered where she was. She sat up in bed, and her heart was beating anxiously in her throat as she glanced about her. The clothes she had worn the previous evening were draped neatly across a chair, but there was no sign of Anton.

Sarah missed him already. She missed the hard warmth of his body in bed beside her, she missed the strength and the feel of those arms which had held her so safely and securely all night, and if this was a taste of what the future had in store for her, then she dreaded it already, but she flung these thoughts aside along with the duvet to dash into the bathroom.

Twenty minutes later she was showered and dressed, her ruined sandals causing her a certain amount of discomfort as she made her way downstairs. Her face was devoid of make-up, but her cotton blouse and skirt were none the worse for the soaking they had received in the storm, and Anton's comb had at least helped to restore order to her tangled hair.

Anton was in the kitchen, dressed in white with his dark hair still damp after his shower and his cheeks clean-shaven. There were scrambled eggs in the pan which stood to one side on the stove, and he was buttering toast when Sarah joined him.

'You're just in time for breakfast,' he smiled, putting down the knife and snaking a possessive arm about her waist.

The fresh, clean smell of his masculine cologne stirred her senses as he tipped up her face to kiss her, but she could not shut her mind to the fact that he would soon be gone.

'You should have woken me earlier,' she admonished him gently when her lips were freed from his lingering kiss. 'I feel guilty about sleeping so late.'

'You were sleeping like a baby, and you looked so beautiful that I didn't have the heart to wake you,' he said, releasing her to remove the plates out of the oven, and dishing a liberal amount of scrambled eggs into each plate. 'I'm starving, so let's eat.'

They ate their breakfast out on the patio where the early morning sunlight filtering through the trees was already showing promise of a sting. The sea was calm after the storm which had ripped along the coast the previous night, and Sarah could see the waves washing out to shore at a lazy pace from where she sat.

'Are you leaving immediately after breakfast?' she questioned Anton when they had disposed of their plates and were drinking their coffee.

'I must leave within the next hour if I want to arrive in Johannesburg before dark this evening.' Anton's features were grave when he met her glance across the table. 'I'll drop you off at the hotel on my way out.'

'That won't be necessary.' She lowered her lashes to veil the sheen of tears in her eyes and raised her cup to her lips to sip at the steaming coffee. 'I'd rather say goodbye here and walk back to the hotel, if you don't mind.'

'Do you have any regrets about last night?'

'No!' She looked up, startled and suddenly anxious that he should ask such a question. 'Have you?'

'None at all,' he smiled, a strange light burning in the depths of his blue eyes as he held her glance. 'Marry me, Sarah.'

Shock drained the colour from her face, leaving her temples pounding, and her cup went down with a clatter, spilling coffee into the saucer and on to her hand.

'*No!*' she cried out in mental as well as physical agony while she dabbed blindly at her hand with a paper serviette.

'No?' he echoed, smiling twistedly, and the air suddenly crackled with tension between them. 'Just like that? No?'

Sarah stared at him, her eyes wide and afraid, and her mind in a chaotic whirl. This wasn't supposed to be happening! He wasn't supposed to be asking her to marry him!

'Marriage is a serious business, Anton,' she said at length, trying desperately to regain control of her faculties.

'You should know, Sarah, that I wouldn't ask you to marry me if I weren't absolutely sure that it would work.'

'But we've only known each other three weeks,' she protested weakly.

'I feel as if I've known you all my life, Sarah.' His hand reached for hers across the table and his fingers gripped hers tightly. 'I know I'm doing this badly,' he said, his voice unsteady with the extent of his feelings. 'This is perhaps not the right place and the right time, but . . . marry me, my love.'

Her throat ached with the tears she dared not shed. Tell him now! her heart wailed. If he loves you then it won't matter that you can't have his children! She considered it, but fear of rejection stilled the words on her tongue.

'I can't!' she cried out despairingly in answer to Anton's proposal and also to her own tormented thoughts as she freed her hand from his and shrank away from him as far as the upright chair would allow. 'I have responsibilities and commitments at Courtney's, and it's a time-consuming task which doesn't allow for marriage.'

'I have responsibilities and commitments where my patients are concerned, and my job is just as time-consuming, but that doesn't mean we can't have a life together.'

'Anton, please, I—it won't work.'

'We could *make* it work, Sarah! I *know* we can!'

Anton was hurting, and so was Sarah. A proposal of marriage from Anton de Ville ought not to be treated lightly, it was an honour he had never bestowed on any other woman before, but Sarah was left with no choice.

'Last night was something special—for both of us—and there'll be other nights, so—let's leave it that way,' she suggested with a calmness she was far from experiencing.

'Confound it, Sarah!' he exploded harshly, his eyes blazing into hers across the table. 'I don't want to have an *affair* with you, I want to *marry* you!'

She shook her head adamantly, the filtered sunlight setting fire to her hair. 'I'm not the right wife for you.'

'What makes you say that?' he demanded, his rugged features taut with anger.

'I just know I'm not the right wife for you. *Please* . . .' She raised her hand in a defensive gesture when he wanted to interrupt her. 'Please, I beg of you, let's not continue with this conversation. Not *now*!'

Anton combed his fingers agitatedly through his hair, and that was all that errant curl needed to fall forward on to his broad forehead. Oh, God, she loved him so much that the pain of it was like a sword being driven into her soul, and her anguish was doubled at the knowledge that she was hurting him too.

'I'll agree to drop the subject on one condition.' His compelling glance captured hers. 'Promise me you'll think it over during this coming week.'

'I promise,' she agreed willingly, knowing that she would be thinking of nothing else, but knowing also that her answer must remain the same.

The tension eased out of Anton's rugged features, but the atmosphere between them was still strained while they finished their coffee. They tried to make conversation, but they failed, and they had both lapsed into an awkward silence when they carried their cups through to the kitchen.

'I'll wash the dishes while you do whatever has to be done before you leave,' Sarah suggested, and was relieved when Anton left the kitchen without making an attempt to reject her offer.

She heard him moving about in the chalet while she washed the dishes, dried them, and stashed them away where they belonged. She heard the Jaguar's boot being slammed shut and car doors being opened and closed while she wiped down the cupboards and the stove, and then Anton's tall, wide-shouldered frame was filling the door into the kitchen.

Their eyes met and held as Sarah draped the cloth over the edge of the sink. It was time for him to leave, and she followed him out of the chalet in silence, waiting for him to lock the door behind them before she accompanied him to where he had parked his dark blue Jaguar.

The sun was warm against her body, but on the inside there was a dreaded coldness seeping into her veins when he opened the door on the driver's side and turned to face her. He trailed a searching, anxious glance over her pale, rigid features, and Sarah felt her throat tighten with tears.

'Sarah . . .' There was uncertainty in his voice and in the touch of his hands when they rested briefly on her shoulders before sliding down along her arms to crush her fingers in their firm clasp. 'You will think about it, won't you?

Sarah swallowed convulsively and nodded. 'I promised,' she reminded him.

He pulled her into his arms, crushing her slender body against his muscled frame while his hard mouth ravaged her soft lips with an almost desperate urgency, and she clung to him a little wildly, wishing that she could hold him to her forever and never let him go, but she had lived too long with the harshness of reality to allow herself the luxury of dwelling on her dreams.

Anton released her moments later with a groan on his lips, and got into his car. 'I'll see you in a week's time,' he said, and then he was driving away up the narrow lane which passed by the hotel.

Sarah watched him go through a blur of tears, and everything suddenly seemed bleak and desolate without Anton's bracing presence. The Jaguar disappeared behind a cluster of flamboyant trees and Sarah lingered outside the chalet, feeling cold and so terribly empty.

She pushed her hands into her skirt pockets and her fingers encountered something papery that crackled when she withdrew it from her pocket. Anton's note! The envelope had a buckled, battered look after being soaked and whirled about in a tumble drier, and Sarah extracted the sheet of paper with trembling fingers.

'I love you, Sarah.' The ballpoint ink had gone a shade paler and it was a little fuzzy, but the words were still there, leaping out at her with an even greater impact than the day before.

The words 'I love you' had been a commitment in themselves, and they were not words which Anton would have used lightly. She should have known this, he had talked often enough about finding the right woman to marry, but yesterday she had been in too much of a mental turmoil to recognise the significance of what he had written.

What would she have done if she had known? Would she have gone to him, or would she have stayed away?

Sarah could not decide. The only thing she was certain of was that if she could have the past twelve hours over again, she would wish to spend them with Anton.

The tears were streaming fast and furiously down her cheeks when she walked up the familiar path to the hotel and, no matter how much she tried, she could not control them. She was still weeping uncontrollably when the hotel building emerged up ahead through the trees, and it was the dreaded thought of being seen that made her hasten towards the side entrance from where she knew she would gain access to her room on the upper floor by way of the service stairs.

Sarah did not emerge from her room until it was time to go down to dinner that evening. Her make-up might have camouflaged the ravages caused by her periodic fits of weeping during the course of that day, but her heart felt leaden and so did her feet.

Would Anton still love her and want her if he knew? Could she risk telling him the truth about herself? Sarah had asked herself those questions over and over again. Her heart was inclined to say, 'Yes', but her mind remained resolute in its decision. It was over, and she had to forget him!

Rose tried to engage her in conversation at the dinner table, but she was only vaguely aware of what Rose was saying, and she was vaguer still about her own responses.

'If you don't feel like talking, then perhaps I could interest you in a game of chess,' Rose tried again with a touch of understandable annoyance when they left the dining-room and retired to the hotel lounge with their coffee.

Sarah was not in the mood for chess, but she agreed.

She tried to shut her mind to everything else except the game as she sat facing Rose across the chess table in a secluded corner of the lounge, but, as the game wore on, she found it increasingly difficult not to let her thoughts wander.

'You're not concentrating, Sarah,' Rose exclaimed accusingly an hour later. 'You've just paved the way for my bishop to capture your queen!'

Sarah leaned back in her chair and closed her eyes for a moment, perilously close to tears, then she smiled wanly into those dark eyes observing her so intently. 'I'm sorry, Rose.'

'You've come to a decision about your relationship with Anton, haven't you?' Rose pounced on the problem with an accuracy which no longer surprised Sarah. 'You spent the night with him, and I sense that it was glorious, but you're not going to see him again.'

The blood surged into Sarah's cheeks and receded again to leave her almost as white as the silk blouse she was wearing with her burgundy-red skirt. Rose's bluntness had stamped her decision with a calculating coldness it did not deserve, and she swallowed convulsively at that aching lump at the back of her throat.

'It's going to hurt, Rose,' she said thickly. 'It's going to hurt like hell, but it will hurt even more if I go on seeing him.'

Rose leaned back in her chair and folded her hands together in her lap, her wizened features bearing the look of a woman who had walked this road before. 'How do you think Anton is going to feel about it?' she asked.

'He'll get over it.'

'Are you sure of that?'

No, I'm not. Sarah bit back that reply and looked away, her eyes dulling with pain. 'I pray with all my heart he does,' she said instead, and she meant it. She did not want to hurt Anton any more than she already had.

'Checkmate!' Rose announced after a lengthy silence, drawing Sarah's attention back to the board in time to see Rose capture her queen and place her king irrevocably in check. 'The game's over, Sarah, but there's one battle which still has to be fought, and I hope you fight it well.'

Sarah did not attempt to understand what Rose was talking about. She swept the chess men into their box, snapped the lid shut, and deposited the box on Rose's side of the table as she rose to her feet with a curt, 'Goodnight.'

What had she expected? What had she hoped for? Sarah asked herself these questions when she lay in bed that night, but the answers continued to evade her.

'I don't want to have an *affair* with you, I want to *marry* you!' Anton had said, and Sarah turned her face into the pillow with a choked cry on her lips.

She had not gone to Anton for the purpose of having an affair with him, but neither had the thought of marriage crossed her mind. The cynical side of her was inclined to suggest that she must have been temporarily deranged to have done something which was so contrary to those rigid principles she had always adhered to, but it was more than that. Much, *much* more!

Her love for Anton was so profound, and so utterly hopeless, that she had allowed herself to be blinded by everything except that driving need to reach out and take whatever he had had to offer her. In retrospect it seemed selfish and callous, but there was nothing selfish and callous about the way she felt at that moment. Anton's proposal had shaken her back to reality and, loving him as much as she did, she could not take her own happiness at his expense.

Sarah knew that this was a sacrifice which would leave yet another deep scar, but it was a sacrifice she had to make, and she would survive the trauma of it as she had survived everything else in her life.

CHAPTER TEN

SARAH watched the earth fall away beneath the Boeing on take-off at Louis Botha Airport, then she leaned back in her seat and sighed inwardly with relief. The last few days at Rosslee had been a nightmare without Anton. She had felt his presence everywhere, tormenting her with memories, and now, at last, she was going home.

'You will keep in touch, won't you?' Sarah recalled Rose's anxious query that morning when they had walked to where the driver of the long-distance taxi service had stood waiting patiently beside his parked vehicle.

'I'll write to you,' Sarah had said, and she intended to keep that promise. Rose Poole was someone she would never forget.

The flight from Durban to Johannesburg took less than an hour, and Sarah arrived at her penthouse shortly after two that Sunday afternoon to find that her cleaning lady had kept everything in perfect order while she had been away.

She left her suitcases in the entrance hall to wander about, drinking in the familiarity of the tastefully furnished rooms, and touching cherished objects. On the dressing-table in her bedroom stood a sleek Siamese cat in fine porcelain with piercing blue eyes. Anton's eyes! Sarah's breath caught in her throat and she withdrew her hand sharply as if the ornamental cat had come alive to claw at her fingers.

'Damm!' The word exploded fiercely from her lips

as she kicked off her navy and white high-heeled shoes. 'I have to forget!' she remonstrated with herself while she exchanged her tailored navy suit for a comfortable cotton housecoat. '*I must* forget!'

She kept herself busy. She unpacked her suitcases, stashed them away, and sorted through her clothes. The wide-brimmed grass hat made her smile, but her smile faded as swiftly as it had appeared. The hat evoked memories of those last few days at Rosslee with Anton, and she flung it into the furthest corner of her cupboard where it would be out of sight.

When she sat in the lounge that evening, sipping coffee and trying to relax, she knew that her life would never be the same again. She had furnished this penthouse with care to make it a comfortable, colourful haven away from the prying eyes of the public, but at that moment it seemed to reflect her own emptiness and desolation.

The chiming of the doorbell made her jump, and her insides shook as she went to answer it. Anton? No! She had fortuitously never given him her address, and no one at Courtney's would pass on that information without her permission. Would they?

Sarah placed her eye up against the peep-hole and smiled with relief as she recognised her godfather's tall, bulky frame on the doorstep. She slid back the security chain and opened the door wide, then she flung herself into Ivor's arms and clung to him with a fervour she had not displayed in years.

'Oh, it's so good to see you again after all these weeks!' she exclaimed, hugging him affectionately.

'You look tanned and rested and absolutely ravishing, my dear,' he said, capturing her hands when she stepped away from him and subjecting her to his smiling, appreciative inspection. 'Your holiday has obviously done you the world of good.'

'I'm more than ready to get back to work in the morning,' she assured him, drawing him inside and closing the door. 'I've a fresh pot of filter coffee brewing. Would you like a cup?'

'A cup of coffee would be most welcome, thank you.' Ivor strolled into the lounge and made himself comfortable in a padded armchair while Sarah took her empty cup through to the kitchen. 'I saw Anton at the club the other night,' he said, drawing on one of the cheroots he occasionally enjoyed and blowing the smoke from his nostrils when Sarah returned to the lounge with their coffee. 'I believe his holiday coincided with yours at Rosslee.'

Sarah's features had settled into a rigid, impenetrable mask as she straightened after placing Ivor's cup of coffee on the glass-topped table within his reach.

'That's correct,' she said, lowering herself gracefully into the cushioned comfort of her chair.

'He didn't say much, but I gathered that the two of you spent quite a lot of time in each other's company.'

'We did,' she responded non-committally, sipping her coffee in too much haste and almost scalding her mouth.

'Anton had planned to meet you at the airport this afternoon, but he called yesterday to tell me that his mother was ill and that he'd be taking the late-night flight down to Cape Town to see her.' The ash had lengthened at the tip of Ivor's cheroot, and he looked vaguely uncomfortable about something as he flicked the ash carefully into the marble ashtray she had placed at his disposal. 'I gave him your telephone number here at the flat, and he'll most probably call you as soon as he returns,' he finally revealed the reason for his discomfiture.

'You shouldn't have done that,' she rebuked him, feeling like an animal whose bolt-hole was in danger of being discovered.

'I know,' Ivor growled in his defence, 'but it seemed the right thing to do at the time.'

Sarah shrugged off her annoyance with a sigh of resignation. She could not blame him for passing on that information, she might have done the same had their circumstances been reversed, and there was no point in upsetting herself about something which she could not alter.

'What's the matter with you, Sarah?' There was agitation in the way Ivor crushed his cheroot into the ashtray, and there was a trace of anger now in the dark eyes which had been observing her so intently for the past few seconds. 'You met Anton while you were on holiday and you spent almost every day in his company, but now that you're home you seem ready to cut all ties with him. If you want me to continue protecting your privacy, Sarah, then you'd better tell me what happened between the two of you at Rosslee.'

Her mask crumbled momentarily to reveal her anguish. 'I fell in love with him, that's what happened.'

'Well, what's so terrible about that?'

'He asked me to marry him.'

Ivor's leathery face creased into a smile. 'But that's wonderful, Sarah!'

'No, it's *not*!'

She stood up abruptly and bit down hard on her

quivering lip as she walked across to the window to stare out across the city with unseeing eyes.

Ivor did not need an explanation, he knew the cause of her deepest sorrow, and he parried her statement grimly with one of his own. 'You haven't told him, have you?'

'No I haven't, and I don't intend to.'

'Oh, my dear, you should.'

'Why?' Sarah turned, her throat working and her facial muscles taut with the effort to suppress that near-physical pain which seemed to be tearing at her very soul. 'Why should I tell him?' she repeated her query in a voice that sounded too harsh to be her own. 'So I can watch him pretend it doesn't matter when I know it does?'

'A man doesn't ask a woman to marry him for the sole purpose of having his children, Sarah,' Ivor tried to reason with her, but Sarah was adamant.

'Anton happens to want children very much, and I don't intend to test the strength of his love for me by dooming him to a childless marriage.'

'My dear girl,' Ivor shook his greying head, 'I think you're making a grave mistake where Anton is concerned, but that's your decision, not mine.'

'You won't tell him, will you?' she demanded sharply, holding her godfather's glance as she returned to her chair and sat down rigidly on the edge of the seat. 'This will remain strictly between us?'

'My lips are sealed, you know that.'

'Thank you.' The words spilled from her lips on an audible sigh, then she steered the conversation abruptly and determinedly away from herself. 'What's been happening while I've been away?'

Ivor obligingly brought her up to date with everything that had happened at Courtney's during her absence, and Sarah fired questions at him, making mental notes and slipping back into her role as business-woman as if the six carefree weeks at Rosslee had never interrupted her working schedule.

She felt optimistic about herself when Ivor left that evening, but a wave of despair engulfed her as she lay alone in her darkened room that night with nothing but the muted sound of the traffic for company. Her work might fill her life again, but there would always be a part of her which would remain empty and desolate without Anton.

Ivor had urged her to take things easy for a while when she returned to work the Monday morning, but Sarah had no desire to sit around idly, and by the end of that first day she was functioning at her usual hectic pace with no time to spare for her own pressing problems.

She had called a meeting for the Wednesday morning of that week, and she was preparing to leave her office when the intercom system buzzed on her desk. She lifted the receiver and jabbed at one of the buttons with a measure of annoyance. 'Yes?' she snapped.

'I know you're on your way out to a meeting, Miss Courtney,' Lois Beecham began apologetically, 'but I have a Dr Anton de Ville on the line, and he says he urgently needs to speak to you.'

Sarah's heart was beating in her throat, but she sounded admirably calm as she said, 'Put him through, Lois.'

There was a soft click as Lois switched the call through, and then the remembered sound of Anton's deep, velvety voice was sending pleasurable little tremors racing through Sarah. 'I believe I've caught you at an inconvenient moment.'

'It doesn't matter.' Her hand shook as she picked up her gold pen and fiddled with it absently. 'How is your mother?'

'She had a mild stroke, but she'll recover from it, and if she tones down her lifestyle she might still live to be a hundred.' There was a brief but tense silence before he asked, 'When am I going to see you, Sarah?'

'I'm not sure,' she prevaricated. 'I'm working to a very tight schedule at the moment.'

'Does that include your evenings?'

'There are several functions which I have to attend.' That was not entirely a lie. There was a fashion show and a photographic exhibition which she had agreed to attend, and then there was a business dinner which she had to sit through with Ivor and their company lawyer.

'What about lunch tomorrow?' Anton persisted.

Sarah searched for an excuse to decline, but then changed her mind. She had to see him once more. She had promised to consider his proposal, and she owed him an answer. All that remained after that would be to make him understand that it was over.

'What time and where?' she asked abruptly, and her expression was strained when she replaced the receiver moments later.

She entered the conference-room three minutes after the specified time to find herself confronted by the curious glances of her clever young assistant, Steve de Vos, and seven other members of her staff. Arriving late for meetings was something which she seldom tolerated in others, and she could not decide whether she ought to be angered or embarrassed by the smiling response she received to her apology.

'I think everyone will agree it's good to know—once in a while—that you're only human like the rest of us,' Steve de Vos elaborated with a teasing smile, and Sarah's sense of humour rose to the fore to save the situation.

'If that's a rap over the knuckles, then I accept it with good grace,' she laughed, and she could sense everyone's approval when she seated herself at the head of the long ebony table. 'Now, let's get down to business.'

That evening, alone at home, Sarah realised that work might be an effective antidote for most things, but it was not powerful enough to rid her mind of Anton. He was there in everything she said and did, punctuating every thought and action with his mockery, his anger, and his loving until her longing for him became a physical ache which she knew she would have to live with for the rest of her life.

She dreaded meeting Anton when she left her office the following day to keep her luncheon appointment with him. Would she sound convincing, or would he see through her act and know that it was false?

The restaurant was crowded, but Sarah saw Anton the instant she entered. His blue eyes drew hers like a magnet tugging forcefully at a pin, and everyone else faded into obscurity as she made her way among the tables towards the man in the pale grey suit who was rising to his feet at her approach. His glance was appreciative as it flicked over her, taking in the amber-coloured silk blouse with the scarf-like collar tied in a casual bow at the base of her throat and the stylish rust-brown skirt and short-sleeved jacket which made her look every inch the successful business-woman she was.

He was smiling at her when they sat facing each other across the small, circular table, and Sarah smiled back at him, but her face felt stiff and her body was rigid with the effort not to reach out and touch him.

'I took the liberty of ordering for us,' Anton explained when a waiter appeared as if out of nowhere to serve them their meal. 'We don't have much time, so I suggest we eat first and talk later.'

Sarah stared down at the smoked salmon and crispy salad on her plate, and her throat ached with tears she dared not shed. She had mentioned once that she preferred a light lunch of smoked salmon and salad, and Anton had remembered. There were so many things she remembered about him too. It was as if he had become an extension of herself, and now she was going to banish him from her life.

She could not recall afterwards whether she had eaten her lunch, or whether her plate had returned untouched to the kitchen, but the cup of aromatic coffee she had ordered was going down well.

'I left you at Rosslee with something to think about,' Anton came straight to the point. 'Did you?'

'I did,' she said, avoiding his probing glance.

'And?'

Sarah was being torn apart on the inside, but she somehow succeeded in remaining outwardly cool and calm as she steeled herself to meet the steady, questioning regard of those piercing blue eyes across the table. 'My answer is still the same.'

His jaw hardened with relentless determination. 'You

might as well know that I intend to do everything within my power to change your mind.'

'You would be wasting your time.'

'Perhaps,' he agreed, 'but I don't give up easily.'

'I see no sense in pursing something which can lead nowhere,' she forced the words past her aching throat. 'What happened between us at Rosslee belongs in the past, and it would simply complicate our lives if we continued to see each other.'

Anton's hand reached for hers, and the crushing grip of his fingers almost made her cry out in agony when he drew her to her feet and ushered her towards the exit.

'What happened between us was something too beautiful and lasting for either of us to crush,' he corrected her harshly when they stood outside the restaurant on the hot, busy pavement. 'I'll see you again, Sarah, and you can count on that.'

He turned on his heel and strode away, leaving her nursing a deep-seated anguish as she watched him disappear amongst the bustling crowd of lunchtime shoppers. What he had said was true, but she had no choice. She had to crush it, for *his* sake more than her own.

Sarah flew down on Cape Town with Ivor towards the end of the following week to inspect the delayed consignment of silk which had arrived at the factory, and they stayed to spend a quiet Christmas at Ivor's cottage in Gordon's Bay.

Those few days away from Johannesburg were a brief respite from the emotional pressure she had had to endure since her last meeting with Anton. As a precaution she had had to turn up the volume of the answering machine at home. She accepted calls only when she was assured that the caller was not Anton, but that did not deter him from calling and leaving messages, asking her to contact him. At the office Lois Beecham knew not to put him through, but to take a message instead.

Sarah never responded to any of those messages, but ignoring them took its emotional toll. She felt reasonably safe at the office, and she knew she could deal with Anton if they should meet unexpectedly in public, but at night, when she left Courtney's and drove herself home, her nervous glance strayed constantly to the rear-view mirror for fear of being followed. It was soul-destroying, and she prayed that Anton would soon tire of the chase.

'I don't give up easily.'

Sarah had cause to remember Anton's warning midway through January. Steve de Vos had been closeted in her office since after lunch on the Friday, reporting on his visit to the various Courtney's stores scattered across the country and offering suggestions for the year ahead.

Sarah made a few demands of her own. 'I want the full winter range on the floor of every Courtney's store before the end of March this year,' she began, 'and I want it advertised well in advance.'

Steve nodded his sleek, fair head. 'I anticipated this, and we're meeting with the advertising company on Tuesday. I see no reason why we shouldn't have——'

The door to Sarah's office was flung open, the accompanying commotion cutting across Steve's reply, and Sarah looked up, annoyed at this unwanted intrusion, to see Anton striding into her office with an indignant, almost frantic Lois Beecham in tow.

Anton's face was a mask of icy, controlled anger, and Sarah's heart lurched uncomfortably in her breast as he stood facing her across the width of her desk.

'I want to speak to you.' His stabbing glance freed Sarah for a moment to shift from Lois Beecham to Steve de Vos, who was rising cautiously to his feet. '*Alone*,' Anton added, and something warned Sarah that it would be unwise to ignore the command in his voice.

'It's all right, Lois, you may go.' Sarah dismissed her secretary with a calmness she was far from experiencing and turned her attention to Steve, who had been regarding the entire incident with undisguised curiosity. 'We'll continue this discussion first thing Monday morning, Steve.'

'Sure,' muttered Steve, collecting his papers in nervous haste and giving Anton's rocklike stature a wide berth to follow Lois Beecham out of the office.

Sarah's emotions were in a painful, chaotic turmoil when the door closed behind them, but she looked outwardly calm as she rose slowly from her chair and walked round her desk to confront Anton. She would rather die than make him aware of the shattering effect his unexpected presence was having on her.

'I assume you have a valid reason for storming unannounced into my office?' she demanded coolly, allowing her glance to linger for a moment on his dark, impeccably tailored suit and striped tie before she met the chilling intensity of his gaze.

'Don't flip the coin with me, Sarah!' he responded cuttingly. 'Your subordinates may be impressed by the ice-machine act, but I'm the man you slept with and made love with six weeks ago, and I happen to know that you're a flesh-and-blood woman with fire instead of ice in your veins.'

'For goodness' sake, lower your voice!' she hissed urgently, her colour coming and going and her heart thudding nervously against her ribs.

'Why?' he demanded with a hint of savagery in his twisted smile. 'Are you ashamed of the fact that we slept together?'

Sarah stared up at him bleakly. 'Please stop it, Anton. Stop hurting yourself and stop hurting me.'

Her words silenced him momentarily, but what ensued was not what she would have wished for. His icy mask disintegrated, and the eyes that held hers suddenly mirrored her own pain and misery.

'I warned you I don't give up easily, but God knows, I've come close to it these past weeks. You don't answer my telephone calls, your home address is a closely guarded secret and, short of spying on you, forcing my way in here seemed the only thing left for me to do.' His voice was low and vibrating with a mixture of pain, frustration and anger. 'Why, Sarah? Why are you doing this to us?'

She lowered her eyes before the probing intensity of his gaze. 'I told you it would be best for both of us if we never saw each other again.'

'You must have a reason for saying that, and I'd like to know what it is.' His expensive leather shoes came into her line of vision, his nearness threatening and emotionally disturbing. 'You'd better tell me, Sarah, because I'm not leaving here until you do.'

Sarah was caught between two conflicting desires, the desire to run and the desire to seek solace in his arms, but she succumbed to neither. 'We can't talk here!' she protested, glancing about her a little wildly. 'Not now!'

Anton gestured angrily with his hands. 'If we can't talk here, then where the devil *can* we talk?'

She stared up at him in silence, her glance resting on the dark hair flecked with grey at the temples, the piercing blue eyes, and the hard, relentless jaw. She wished she could smooth away the angry frown creasing his brow and the tightness about his sensuous mouth, but she dared not grant herself that privilege.

There's one battle which still has to be fought, and I hope you fight it well. Rose's words leapt unbidden into Sarah's mind, and their meaning was suddenly perfectly clear. This was the final battle, and recognising that fact sent a blessed numbness surging into her.

She turned away and, lifting the telephone receiver to her ear, jabbed a finger on the appropriate button. 'Please cancel my appointments for this afternoon, Lois.' She replaced the receiver and turned back to Anton, sealing her fate with a calm, 'We'll go to my penthouse.'

Anton had followed Sarah so closely in his Jaguar that she had been afraid he might ram into the back of her Mercedes when she had been forced to slam on the brakes to avoid a collision with a vehicle which had swerved out of a parking bay directly into her path. It was as if he had feared that she might want to avoid this confrontation by losing him in the traffic, but Sarah had set herself on a path along which there was no return. She had to go through to the bitter end despite the knowledge of the pain and suffering which awaited her.

She was in the grip of a deadly calmness when they stepped out of the lift which had swept them up to the penthouse of the luxury flats where she lived. Anton was the only man, other than her godfather, to be invited across the threshold to her private sanctum, and she knew that the memory of his presence between these walls would linger hauntingly, but she brushed this knowledge aside as she unlocked the door and led the way inside.

Anton closed the door behind them and glanced about him with interest while he discarded his jacket and loosened his collar and tie. Sarah observed him unobtrusively, recalling vividly the texture of his skin against her palms, but then her mind was forging ahead relentlessly to the things which had to be said between them.

'Would you like something to drink?' she offered absently, placing her briefcase on the carpeted floor beside the telephone table and straightening as she turned to face him.

'I suggest we talk first.' His narrowed gaze flicked over her pale, rigid features and the breath left his lips in an impatient hiss as he breached the gap between them in one long stride. 'Perhaps the talking could wait as well.'

He had moved so swiftly that Sarah was caught off her guard, and she knew it would be futile to attempt to free herself from those steely arms crushing her slender body against his hard frame. His mouth swooped down on hers before she could utter a sound and, despite her efforts to the contrary, she found herself responding to the searing hunger of his kiss.

The blood was singing in her veins, and she was trembling and clinging weakly to his wide shoulders when he finally eased his mouth from hers to seek out that pulsating hollow at the base of her throat. She had wanted to avoid this; she had known it could make matters so much more difficult for her, but . . . oh, God . . . how she had needed it!

Anton's warm, sensuous mouth against the sensitive cord of her throat was a delicious torment, and every nerve and sinew in her body seemed to quiver in delightful anticipation as his hands slid up beneath her cotton jacket to stroke the smooth skin above the waistline of her skirt.

'Marry me, Sarah,' he murmured close to her ear, and the sobering effect of those words was like a savage electrical charge jolting her insides.

'I can't!' The words came out on an anguished cry as she pushed him away from her and put the width of the room between them to lean against the ornamental fireplace with her hands gripping the mantelshelf. 'I *can't* marry you!'

'*Why* can't you?' he demanded with a harshness that scraped painfully across her sensitive, throbbing nerves. '*Confound* it, Sarah, why won't you *trust* me?'

'I *do* trust you! I'd trust you with my life, but—oh, God!' Her voice cracked and she shuddered with the effort to control herself, but her eyes were dark pools of undisguised pain in her white face when she turned to him. 'There's something I must tell you.'

'Sarah . . .' His expression was grave as he took a pace towards her, but he halted in his stride when she raised her hands in an urgent gesture of appeal.

'Please let me finish before my—my courage deserts me,' she pleaded huskily, lowering her hands and lacing her fingers together so tightly that they ached. 'I was three months pregnant when I was involved in the accident I told you about,' she began, steeling herself inwardly. 'The injuries I received were so severe that I lost the baby as well as the ability to have another. So you see,' she added dully, 'that's why I can't marry you. I can't give you the children you want so much, and the reason why I've never told you this before was because I—I couldn't bear the thought of your rejection, but now . . .' Her shoulders sagged tiredly and she gestured despairingly with her hands. 'Now I simply want to get it over with.'

Sarah felt barren in mind and body during the ensuing silence, and she had no way of guessing what lay behind Anton's inscrutable expression when he walked towards her. She was like a carton, emptied of its contents and worthless, and all that remained was for Anton to tell her so.

'I know you can't have children,' he said, his voice low and throaty with emotion, and his eyes mirroring her pain as if it were his own as he led her to the sofa and drew her down beside him. 'I've known from the very beginning,' he added gently.

Sarah stared at him blankly for several seconds before his words penetrated the mental shield she had erected to ward off the agony of his rejection. The room seemed to tilt around her as the stunning implication of his statement finally hit her, and her heart missed several suffocating beats, making her appreciate the fact that she was seated when she felt that odd weakness surging into her limbs.

'You *know*?' she demanded stupidly, her eyes dilated and her temples pounding. 'But how—who told you?'

Anton's ruggedly handsome features softened into a

smile. 'You obviously don't remember, but you gave me the name and address of your doctor in Cape Town, and he passed your medical history on to me when I requested it.'

'I didn't know that.'

'Not many people do, but it's common procedure among medical practitioners when they need to make a complete diagnosis.'

Sarah stared down at those strong hands clasping hers and shook her head in a visible attempt to clear her mind before she met his probing glance. 'Why didn't you tell me you knew?'

'At first it was simply a medical fact which didn't relate to your condition at the time, and it remained unimportant even when I knew I was falling in love with you, but I plead guilty to a certain stubbornness when I realised that you were making an issue of it by refusing to marry me.' His fingers tightened painfully about hers as if to convey his own anguish. 'I wanted you to love me and trust me enough to give me that information of your own free will.'

Sarah did not doubt him, the truth was there in his eyes and in his touch, but she was still too confused and bewildered to grasp it. 'You've known all this time that I can't have a child, and you still want to marry me?' she demanded incredulously.

'Why should you find that so difficult to accept?'

'But you want children! You *said* so!' she cried, wrenching her hands free of his to pound his chest with her fists in frustration and despair.

'I know I did,' he laughed suddenly, capturing her hands and imprisoning them against his chest. 'I was prodding you in the hope that you'd confide in me.'

'Are you asking me to believe that you don't really want children of your own?' she demanded, disbelief flashing in the eyes she raised to his, and he shook his head, his expression sobering.

'I wouldn't insult your intelligence by asking you to believe a lie. What I want you to believe is that you're the woman I want to share the rest of my life with. I can live without having a child of my own, but I can't bear the thought of living without you. I love you, Sarah.'

There was no pretence with Anton, only a quiet sincerity, and it touched her deeply, allaying her fears. 'I love you too,' she managed in a shaky whisper, her eyes brimming with tears of mingled relief and joy. 'That's why I thought we shouldn't see each other again.'

'You're in my blood, my love.' His voice was vibrating with an emotion she had never heard before as he pressed her hands flat against his chest so that she could feel the steady thudding of his heart through his shirt. 'You're the pulse of my very existence, and there can never be anyone else.'

'Oh, Anton! Darling, I love you so much!'

She smiled at him through her tears, her joy almost too much to bear, and then she was in his arms, clinging to him and responding a little wildly to his kisses.

'I deserve to be compensated for the agony you've put me through these past six weeks,' Anton growled when passion flared between them.

'I could do with a certain amount of compensation myself,' Sarah countered with a provocative smile, thrilling to the fires that leapt in his eyes as she drew him to his feet and led him into her bedroom.

She was free at last. She had fought the final battle

and, incredibly, she had won.

A few days later Rose Poole received a long letter from Sarah with an invitation to attend her marriage to Anton.

'Checkmate,' Rose muttered gleefully as she went into the hotel lobby to book her flight to Johannesburg.

THE ROMANCE THAT STARTED IT ALL!

For Diane Bauer and Nick Granatelli, the walk down the aisle was a rocky road....

Don't miss the romantic prequel to WITH THIS RING—

I THEE WED
BY ANNE McALLISTER

Harlequin American Romance #387

Let Anne McAllister take you to Cambridge, Massachusetts, to the night when an innocent blind date brought a reluctant Diane Bauer and Nick Granatelli together. For Diane, a smoldering attraction like theirs had only one fate, one future—marriage. The hard part, she learned, was convincing her intended....

Watch for Anne McAllister's I THEE WED, available *now* from Harlequin American Romance.

ITW

HARLEQUIN'S WISHBOOK
SWEEPSTAKES RULES & REGULATIONS
NO PURCHASE NECESSARY TO ENTER OR RECEIVE A PRIZE